P9-CJR-333

SHAKESPEARE'S SECRET

SHAKESPEARE'S SECRET

✦ ✦ ✦ ELISE BROACH ✦ ✦ ✦

HENRY HOLT AND COMPANY ✦ NEW YORK

Henry Holt and Company, LLC
Publishers since 1866
115 West 18th Street, New York, New York 10011
www.henryholt.com

Henry Holt is a registered trademark of Henry Holt and Company, LLC

Distributed in Canada by H. B. Fenn and Company Ltd.

Library of Congress Cataloging-in-Publication Data
Broach, Elise. Shakespeare's secret / Elise Broach.—1st ed.
p. cm.
Summary: Named after a character in a Shakespeare play, misfit sixth-grader Hero becomes interested in exploring this unusual connection because of a valuable diamond supposedly hidden in her new house, an intriguing neighbor, and the unexpected attention of the most popular boy in school.
ISBN-13: 978-0-8050-7387-4
ISBN-10: 0-8050-7387-6
1. Shakespeare, William, 1564–1616—Authorship—Juvenile fiction. [1. Shakespeare, William, 1564–1616—Authorship—Fiction. 2. Great Britain—History—Henry VIII, 1509–1547—Fiction. 3. Great Britain—History—Elizabeth, 1558–1603—Fiction. 4. Mystery and detective stories. 5. Neighbors—Fiction. 6. Maryland—Fiction.] I. Title.
PZ7.B78083Sh 2005 [Fic]—dc21 2004054020

First edition—2005 / Book designed by Donna Mark
Printed in the United States of America on acid-free paper. ∞

1 3 5 7 9 10 8 6 4 2

Permission for use of the following is gratefully acknowledged:

Portrait of Edward de Vere on page 246 courtesy of Mary Evans Picture Library.

"Do Not Go Gentle Into That Good Night" by Dylan Thomas, from *The Poems of Dylan Thomas,* copyright © 1952 by Dylan Thomas. Reprinted by permission of New Directions Publishing Corp.

"I'm Nobody! Who are you?" by Emily Dickinson, reprinted by permission of the publishers and the Trustees of Amherst College from *The Poems of Emily Dickinson,* Thomas H. Johnson, ed., Cambridge, Mass.: The Belknap Press of Harvard University Press, Copyright © 1951, 1955, 1979, 1983 by the President and Fellows of Harvard College.

For my parents,
Barbara and Bill Broach

SHAKESPEARE'S SECRET

CHAPTER 1

It was the last day of summer. Hero Netherfield stretched across the quilted bedspread in her sister's room, her feet drifting over the edge of the mattress. She wasn't thinking about their new house. She wasn't thinking about school. She wasn't thinking about stepping off the bus tomorrow into a sea of strangers. If she thought about any of those things, she'd get that old, tight, panicky feeling—and what was the point?

So instead, she rested her cheek against the soft cotton and breathed. The air was thick with summer smells: lawn clippings and suntan lotion and late-blooming roses. She could hear the distant shouts of a tag game down the street. She closed her eyes and made her mind completely blank, as heavy and blank as the summer day.

It took a lot of concentration. Too much. After a minute, she rolled on her side and said to her sister, "You got the best room."

Beatrice's room in the new house was full of angles and alcoves, like Hero's, but it was bigger, with more windows. Beatrice had hung posters on the sloping ceiling, and they floated colorfully overhead, like the inside flaps of a circus tent.

Her sister sat at the desk with one foot propped on an open drawer. She painted her toenails with quick, smooth strokes. "So?" she said. "It was my turn."

That was true. They took turns choosing bedrooms every time they moved, and Hero had chosen first at the house in New York.

"You have a good room, too," Beatrice said. "You just need to put stuff up on the walls."

"Yeah, I know." Hero sighed. But what? She'd finally opened the moving boxes from her old bedroom yesterday. They were filled with stuffed animals, seashells, crunched wildlife posters, all the things she'd collected since she was five. She wasn't sure she even recognized that person anymore. None of it belonged in the room of a sixth-grader. A little wistfully, she'd packed it all up again and shoved the boxes in one of the closets under the eaves. That was the strange thing about moving so often. It forced you to think about starting over every time, whether you wanted to or not.

The only things Hero kept out for her new room were her books and a shoe box of antique bottles she'd found at a garage sale, colorful glass vials that once held medicine, hair tonic, maybe perfume. The books she wedged into the dark corner bookcases, stacking a pile of favorites next to her bed. The bottles she arranged in a cluster on the window seat, thinking about all the places they must have been, all the hands that must have held them. She liked the way they caught the sunlight and scattered soft shadows of green and lavender on the floor. But the walls themselves were still completely bare. Hero couldn't think of anything to hang on them.

She rolled onto her stomach and covered her face with her hands. "I can't believe that school starts tomorrow."

"Me neither." Beatrice fanned her toenails. "But maybe it won't be so bad this time."

"It never is bad for *you,* Triss."

Sometimes it amazed Hero that she and her sister were actually part of the same family. When she was little, she used to suspect she was adopted, an idea that struck her as both upsetting and exotic—and somehow much easier to believe than the truth.

Beatrice was tall and pretty, with wavy reddish hair and an open, sunny face. She always seemed about to smile, if she wasn't already smiling. Hero, on the other hand, was small and dark. Without meaning to, she wore a worried look much of the time. At the grocery store or the mall, complete strangers would touch her arm and ask sympathetically, "What's the matter, honey? Don't you feel well?"

At school tomorrow, Hero knew exactly what would happen. After a brief sizing-up, Beatrice would be swept into a throng of would-be friends, girls who'd show her the restrooms, save her a place in the cafeteria, share their phone numbers and e-mail addresses. They'd admire her hair, they'd compliment her nail polish. By the end of tomorrow—even though it was only her first day—Beatrice would fit in. Her plans for the weekend would include half the eighth grade.

For Hero, it would be a different story entirely. She'd still be the new kid months from now. She flinched when she thought of what lay ahead: figuring out the lockers, the right clothing to wear, the acceptable food to pack for lunch. Every school had its own customs and fashions, and if she wanted to blend in, she never had long to find out what they were. It was such hard work, Hero thought: that constant, draining effort to slip into the crowd unnoticed. "Blending in" was completely different than "fitting in." It was the difference between camouflaging yourself in the forest and actually being one of the trees.

"Oh, come on, Hero," Beatrice said. "Maryland is almost the South. People seem friendlier here." She laughed suddenly. "Besides, last year everything worked out okay. You had Kate and Lindsey."

"Ugh!" Hero made a face. "Kate and Lindsey. That was totally not worth it."

Kate and Lindsey had been her friends in fifth grade. They had identical blond ponytails and high-pitched, unstoppable squeals. Hero had nothing in common with them. It still amazed her that they'd ended up spending so much of the last year together. It was a relationship based purely on need. Kate and Lindsey, struggling not to fail Language Arts, had needed a third person to help with their Greek myths skit. They chose Hero, who ended up writing the whole play while the two of them huddled together and whispered about their one consuming interest, a boy named Jeremy Alexander. They stalked Jeremy throughout the school day (without ever actually talking to him) and then spent hours in endless, inconclusive conversations about whether he even knew they existed.

In return for putting up with this, Hero found herself with a lifeline of sorts. She had someone to sit with at lunch, to hang out with at recess, and to join for team activities in gym. Of course, if the game ever called for partners, it was understood that the pair would be Kate and Lindsey, and Hero would be on her own.

"They were awful," Beatrice said, still laughing. "Remember how obsessed they were with that boy?"

"Remember? That was my life." Hero raised her voice several octaves. "*He looked at me!* Did not! *Did too! In Social Studies!* Sideways or did he turn his whole head? *Whole head!* No way!"

Beatrice mimicked their earsplitting scream. "Remember how Dad always used to forget Lindsey's name?" she asked.

Hero smiled. "He called them 'Kate and the other Kate.' How could he forget a regular name like Lindsey?"

Beatrice shrugged. "It didn't come from Shakespeare."

Hero and Beatrice were both named for characters in the play *Much Ado About Nothing*, thanks to the English literature class where their parents met in college. Naturally, Beatrice had gotten the familiar name, one that lent itself to bouncy nicknames like

Trixie, or Bea, or Triss. Hero's name was inevitably misunderstood, questioned, and laughed at. For several months at the last school, one of her teachers had called her Nero.

Of course, she hadn't told her parents that. Her mother loved Shakespeare, but her father actually lived it. It was his job. For as long as Hero could remember, he'd been reading, studying, and writing about Shakespeare. When she was little, she used to wake up in the middle of the night to the sound of his voice floating through the darkness. She would pad through the sleeping house to find him, usually at the dining-room table, hunched over the wings of a book, reading out loud. He would always let her listen for a while before he carried her back to bed. The words didn't make any sense—Hero never understood what was happening—but the language was musical and full of feeling. She liked sitting in the dim room and hearing the rhythm of it.

Her father's years in graduate school and a string of teaching and research jobs had taken them from Illinois to Massachusetts to New York, and finally here to Maryland, where he would be working as an archivist at the Maxwell Elizabethan Documents Collection in Washington, D.C. When the whole family had visited the library last week, Hero thought its stained-glass windows and vaulted ceilings made it look like a cathedral. It was filled with books and long, shining wood tables. There were glass cases everywhere, which held old, curling brown manuscripts.

"Dad seems to love that Maxwell place," she said to Beatrice. "And everybody there looks just like him. Sort of rumpled and tweedy."

"Yeah," Beatrice said. "Even the women have beards. It's perfect for him."

It was amazing to think of a place that was perfect for their father. He was so weird, and not just in the way all parents were weird. He used words like "Fie" and "tetchy," and he could quote long passages from Shakespeare by heart. He never did the things that other dads did, like play golf or watch football on TV. He had no idea how to grill a steak. But Beatrice was right: Compared to the rest of the staff at the Maxwell, he seemed normal.

"Do you think that's how it is for everybody?" Hero asked. "Do you think even the weirdest people seem normal if you put them in the right place?"

Beatrice thought for a minute. "Are you talking about Dad or yourself?"

Hero grabbed the pillow and hurled it at her, almost knocking over the nail polish.

"Hey!" Beatrice said. "I was just kidding. Relax, school will go fine tomorrow. You worry too much."

Hero shook her head. "No, I don't. When you're me, it's not possible to worry too much."

At that moment, their mother appeared in the doorway. She was holding a large pair of pruning shears, and her cheeks were streaked with sweat. From the expression on her face, they could tell she'd been listening.

"Well," she said to Hero, "I suppose if you worry *too* much, you'll always be pleasantly surprised."

Hero's mother was the kind of steady, cheerful person who was determined to find hidden advantages in the most unlikely situations. She did graphic design work, mostly freelance because they moved so often, and she knew all the differences between typefaces with funny names like Garamond and Desdemona. Even in her work, she never seemed to have a bad day. Sometimes Hero longed for her to be bored and depressed just so they'd have something in common.

"Please, Hero," her mother said. "Don't spend the whole day feeling sorry for yourself. It's beautiful outside. Do me a favor and run these clippers back to Mrs. Roth."

"Aw, Mom," Hero protested. Mrs. Roth was the old woman who lived next door. Hero had seen her outside in her overgrown garden, but she'd never spoken to her. "I don't even know her. Make Triss do it."

"No, I want you to do it. This will be a chance for you to get to know her." Her mother leaned the shears against the doorjamb and disappeared down the hallway.

For a minute longer, Hero lay staring at the ceiling, at the cracks and water stains, and at the old glass light fixture with its pattern of vines and flowers. Out of the corner of her eye, she could see that Beatrice was now painting her fingernails, brushing shimmering layers of pink over each one.

"What color is that?" she asked indifferently.

"'Ballet Slipper.' Do you like it?"

"I guess."

"Want to try it?" Beatrice brightened. "I could give you a makeover."

Hero rolled her eyes. Beatrice had a book called *The Sum of Your Parts* that was full of advice on how to highlight your best features. According to Beatrice, Hero's best features were her dark eyes and her long brown hair. They were just begging to be accentuated in a makeover.

"No way," Hero said, sliding to her feet. "Then I'll look totally different tomorrow, and the next day when I look like myself, everyone will go, 'Ew! What happened to her?'" She picked up the pruning shears. "Besides, it's the last day of summer vacation and apparently Mom wants me to spend it with a total stranger."

Sighing, she tripped lightly down the stairs, flung open the screen door, and stepped into the blaze and trill of the summer day.

CHAPTER 2

Mrs. Roth's house was a yellow cottage with peeling paint, a wide porch, and a dense, colorful front garden. There were flowers everywhere, clusters of roses, bright pockets of marigolds, petunias, geraniums, snapdragons. But the flowers tumbled out of a mound of weeds and thistles. Hero picked her way gingerly along the flagstone walk, the hard metal pruning shears banging her leg. She hesitated in front of the porch steps, eyeing the thick shrubbery on either side. It almost blocked her path. Why, she wondered, had her mother even thought to ask Mrs. Roth for pruning shears? It didn't look like they'd ever been used in this yard.

"Mrs. Roth?" Hero called out, hoping to avoid actually knocking on the door. Maybe she could just leave the clippers on the porch. She didn't particularly want to be drawn into a conversation, or, worse yet, invited inside. She never felt comfortable around old people. She didn't like their papery skin, or the way they always launched into long, pointless anecdotes.

To her dismay, Hero heard footsteps approaching the door.

"I brought back your pruning shears," she called, dropping the clippers on the porch. "Thanks a lot."

She turned and started to jog back over the flagstones, but the door swung open and a voice called out, "You're very welcome. Tell your mother she may borrow them anytime."

Hero answered over her shoulder, "Okay, thanks, I will."

She was almost to the gate when she realized unhappily that the old woman was coming down the front steps into the garden.

"Now, let's see . . . are you the younger daughter?" Mrs. Roth asked.

Defeated, Hero turned around. She walked back a few paces and awkwardly held out her hand.

"Yes," she said. "I'm Hero."

Mrs. Roth stood in the middle of her unkempt garden, thin and strangely elegant looking. Hero noticed that she wore a long-sleeved blouse and trousers despite the sticky heat. Her hand was cool and she shook Hero's firmly. She had short silver hair cropped closely around her face, and her blue eyes were full of friendly interest.

"Hero. Yes, of course. Your sister is Beatrice, isn't she? *Much Ado About Nothing*. Hero's a lovely name. 'Who can blot that name with any just reproach?'"

She's as weird as Dad, Hero realized.

Mrs. Roth smiled. "It's from the play. You've read it, haven't you?"

Hero shook her head. "Uh, no."

Of course that's what people always assumed, since she was the daughter of a Shakespeare expert. But she'd never read any of the plays herself. Never wanted to. That was her father's specialty. As far as Hero was concerned, it belonged to him completely. In families, things seemed to get sorted out that way. It was like choosing tokens in a board game. Her father got Shakespeare. Beatrice got popularity. Her mother got good humor. You could never have two people share the same token. That would be too confusing.

But Mrs. Roth looked disappointed. "Oh, you must read it, it's wonderful. Of course, Beatrice is the stronger character, witty and resourceful. Hero's just a pretty fluff. But she is honorable. That's the point. And it's an excellent name to live up to."

"I guess." Hero looked away uncertainly. "Well, I'd better get going."

"Why don't you take some flowers with you? I have so many. They could stand to be cut back a bit."

"Oh, that's okay." Hero could see that Mrs. Roth was already walking purposefully toward the house.

"I'll just fetch a pair of scissors. You'll have to cut them yourself, if you don't mind. My arthritis keeps me from doing much gardening, I'm afraid."

Hero shifted from one foot to the other, trying to think of some excuse that would justify a speedy exit.

But a minute later, Mrs. Roth returned with the scissors. She directed Hero toward the roses. "I'm Miriam, by the way."

Hero couldn't imagine ever calling her that, but she tried to smile politely. She drew back the prickly stems and began clipping the rosebushes, tossing the heavy blossoms on the walkway. Mrs. Roth hovered behind her and gathered the flowers into a loose bouquet.

"Has school started yet?" she asked.

"No," Hero said. "Tomorrow."

"And what grade are you entering?"

"Sixth. Beatrice is in eighth."

"It must be difficult for you, adjusting to a new school."

Hero snorted at the understatement before she caught herself. "Yeah, it is, sometimes. But I guess I'll find out tomorrow."

She passed a last handful of roses to Mrs. Roth and straightened. "That's enough, isn't it?" She was beginning to think she'd be stuck here until the school bus came tomorrow morning.

Mrs. Roth lowered her face into the armful of petals and inhaled. "Yes, that's plenty. You'll have trouble finding a vase large enough to hold them."

She gave the roses to Hero, studying her thoughtfully. "Good luck tomorrow at school. It's been such a pleasure to meet your family. Arthur Murphy, the man who used to live in your house, told me he'd found the perfect new owners for it. I can see exactly what he meant. He wouldn't sell to just anyone, you know. That house was very special to him."

Hero glanced over her shoulder at the gate. "My mom and dad said he was really nice to them."

"Oh, he was very impressed with your father. A Shakespeare scholar! Arthur's wife was English, and they were both quite literary."

Hero nodded. "Well, I should go."

"Of course," Mrs. Roth said. "With school starting, you probably have lots to do. Let me open the gate for you." She swung it wide and seemed about to step out of the way, but then she paused. "You know, Hero, when you meet your classmates tomorrow, if you need something to break the ice, you might tell them that you're living in the Murphy diamond house. That will make you something of a celebrity."

Hero lowered the thorny stems to look at her. "What do you mean?"

"Your house," Mrs. Roth repeated. "Your parents know the story, don't they? I thought the Realtor would have told them. Most people around here believe that the house has a diamond hidden in it. A seventeen-carat one, somewhere on the property."

"A diamond? You're kidding."

"No, not at all. It was quite a scandal last year. The police, the insurance company—everyone got involved."

Hero shook her head. "I don't get it. Why would anyone hide something so valuable?"

"Well—" Mrs. Roth began, but at that moment they heard Beatrice's voice from the Netherfields' back porch.

"Hero! Hero, Mom needs you."

Hero frowned. "Okay, coming," she called. She looked at Mrs. Roth. "Maybe you could tell me the rest of the story some other time."

"Of course. Stop by after school tomorrow if you like. I'd be happy to tell you about it."

Hero nodded. Holding the roses gingerly, she negotiated her way through the gate and started toward home. "Bye, Mrs. Roth," she called. "Thanks for the flowers."

"Good-bye, Hero. I'll see you soon."

Hero glanced over her shoulder. She could see Mrs. Roth moving through the wild tangle of garden, tenderly lifting the blossoms.

CHAPTER 3

As the school bus pulled into the long drive, Hero craned for a closer look at the blank, brick side of Ogden Elementary. It was only eight thirty in the morning, but the air was so soupy and hot that her thighs stuck to the vinyl seat. She felt vaguely sick to her stomach, just as she had all morning, too worried even to think about eating breakfast. At the kitchen table earlier, her mother's encouraging glances and her father's hearty enthusiasm had only made her feel worse.

Beatrice had left an hour ago for junior high, gotten a ride, of course, with a girl who lived three blocks away. Hero felt a pang of pure envy. This wouldn't be nearly so bad if she had somebody, anybody, to walk in with her. But at the bus stop that morning, the neighborhood crowd had sized her up sullenly and quickly sorted itself into small bunches of kids talking and comparing backpacks. Hero had been left to stand with a little boy who was starting first grade. To her chagrin, he seemed to take an immediate liking to her and chattered nonstop. His name was Aaron, he was losing his bottom tooth ("This one right here!"), he'd been to a Baltimore Orioles game on Saturday ("It was great!"), and his dad got him a hat, but hats weren't allowed in school so he was just going to wear it on the bus.

Now he was leaning over the back of the seat in front of her, looking anxious. "Can you take me to my classroom?"

"Don't you know where it is?"

"I think so. But I don't remember how to go."

Hero sighed. "I guess."

The bus rumbled to a stop in front of the school, and the seats emptied in a flurry. The bigger boys jostled their way to the front, their backpacks swinging through the air. Aaron, twisting his Orioles hat, hung back, and Hero felt obliged to stay with him. They were the last to get off the bus.

In the lobby, she grabbed his hand and they stood for a minute, resisting the press of moving bodies, looking around. The main corridor echoed with laughter and noise. The walls were painted a dull green, and beige-flecked linoleum tile covered the floor, stretching in all directions. It looked institutional, like a hospital or prison. The overall effect was completely bland and vaguely threatening at the same time.

Hero glanced down at Aaron. "What's your room number?"

Aaron's brow furrowed. "Um . . . it has an 8 in it."

"Oh, come on, don't you even—" Hero exclaimed, but she stopped herself. Aaron seemed about to cry.

"It's okay," she said. "We'll find it."

Finding it turned out to be more complicated than Hero expected. It meant a visit to the office, then a detour to the first-grade wing, then her own long-distance sprint to the opposite end of the school, where the sixth-grade classrooms were. She paused outside the closed door of Mrs. Vanderley's room, knowing with a terrible, sinking certainty that she was late. She could hear the low murmur of the students inside, broken by the teacher's staccato announcements. She took a deep breath, squared her shoulders, and walked in.

As Hero suspected, the other kids were already in their seats. The teacher looked up in surprise when the door opened.

"I'm sorry I'm late," Hero mumbled, quickly scanning the room for an empty desk.

"Oh hello, you're new, aren't you?" the teacher said, smiling. "I'll introduce you to the rest of the class. Let's see, your name is . . ." Mrs. Vanderley studied the attendance roster, pursing her lips. Here we go, thought Hero.

"It's Hero," she said, her voice ringing in the quiet classroom. "Hero Netherfield."

"Hero?" said a red-haired girl in the front row. "Hey, that's my dog's name."

The words seemed to spill into the air and stay there, frozen, like the speech bubble in a cartoon. For a moment, Hero hoped against hope that no one had heard. But a split second later the classroom erupted in laughter. Not snickers or muffled giggles but a great rolling roar. Two boys in the back began whistling and slapping their jeans, calling, "Here, Hero, here, girl!"

Someone else yelled, "Watch out, she's not house-broken!" Hero felt her cheeks burn. She stared at the floor.

Mrs. Vanderley seemed momentarily at a loss. She looked at Hero and at the class with equal annoyance. Then she thumped her hand on the desk.

"That's enough! That is *enough*. Hero, why don't you sit at this desk in the front? I want all of you to take out your spelling notebooks."

Hero hurried across the room and slid into the empty seat. She searched her backpack for her notebook, trying to look like she didn't care, like this kind of thing happened all the time. But her heart filled with despair. There was no way the dog joke would end here. It was exactly the kind of mindless label that stuck to a person like glue. In this class, in this school, she would always be the girl named after a dog.

⋄ ⋄ ⋄

The rest of the day did nothing to make her feel better. All morning, she could hear furtive whispered commands like "Down, girl" and "Roll over." In the hall on the way to the art room, several boys whistled softly. Back at her desk, she found a torn strip of notebook paper with "woof" scrawled across it.

Lunch was even worse. Hero threaded her way through the crowded, noisy cafeteria to an empty table, only to have a small posse of kids surround her as soon as she sat down.

"You can't sit there. That's our table," a thin blond girl told her.

"Yeah," another girl added. "You're in Kendra's seat."

Hero looked at them doubtfully. She was pretty sure there weren't assigned seats, but if they wanted her to move, it didn't really matter.

"Sorry," she mumbled. She picked up her tray and slid into a seat at the end of a long table nearby. But the kids there immediately began making barking noises.

For the entire day, her only small consolation was that the red-haired girl who'd started the whole thing clearly felt as embarrassed about the teasing as Hero did. When the bell rang at dismissal, they ended up next to each other in the bus line.

The red-haired girl said softly, "I wish I hadn't said that about my dog. I didn't know they'd start teasing you about it."

Hero looked away. "Yeah . . . how could you know?"

"The thing is," the girl continued, "he's a really great dog. That's why we named him Hero."

Hero hoisted her backpack over her shoulder. She knew the girl was trying to apologize. She knew she should say something to make it easier. But she felt completely empty, as if every ounce of thoughtfulness and courtesy had been sucked right out of her.

"I guess it does make a good dog's name," she said at last, and then hurried outside to the bus.

She had never wanted to go home so badly in her entire life. Her whole body longed for it. At least the nausea she'd felt that morning, the waves of fretful anticipation, had disappeared. Every time her family moved she had a brief spell of imagining that the new school might be different, that here she would somehow reinvent herself and end up accepted, liked, even popular. Sometimes that small bubble of hope lingered for weeks. This time, even though the bubble had burst, at least it had all happened quickly.

Hero climbed onto the bus. Aaron was waving his baseball cap at her. As she settled into the seat behind him, she thought for the first time that day about Mrs. Roth, who was expecting her to stop by on the way home.

CHAPTER 4

The school bus groaned to a halt at the street corner. Hero hurried down the steps and jumped lightly to the sidewalk. Three older boys stood in an intimidating huddle at the street sign, and she ducked her head as she walked past.

"Bye, Hero," Aaron yelled, racing toward his front yard. Hero started to call out to him, but she noticed the boys were watching her, so instead she lifted one arm to wave. The junior high bus must have come a while ago. Beatrice would be home already.

Until Hero reached the edge of Mrs. Roth's yard, she hadn't fully decided whether or not to stop. She wanted to hear about the diamond. But she felt so battered by the school day that she wasn't sure she had the energy to be with anyone, even if all she had to do was listen. But then, as she glanced at the lush jungle of flowers, she saw Mrs. Roth sitting on her front stoop, reading the newspaper. Again she was dressed in a crisp blouse and long pants, oblivious to the wilting heat.

Hero stopped at the gate. "Hi," she called uncertainly.

Mrs. Roth looked up. "Well, hello! I didn't realize it was so late. How was your first day?"

Hero shrugged. "Pretty much the same as always. A little worse, maybe."

Mrs. Roth looked at her for a minute, then patted the step. "Come sit down," she said. "You can help me with the crossword. Then I'll keep my promise and tell you about the Murphy diamond."

The wooden boards of the porch were warm from the sun and creaked agreeably as Hero sat down. Mrs. Roth spread the newspaper between them, handing Hero the pen she was holding.

"Five letters, *exhausted,*" she said. "There's a *y* at the end."

"Weary," said Hero promptly.

"Oh, yes, excellent. Fill it in."

Hero carefully wrote the word in block letters. She scanned the remaining clues.

"Eight letters, *one who hopes,*" she read.

"Optimist," said Mrs. Roth.

They took turns with the pen until the puzzle was almost complete. Then Mrs. Roth slid the paper onto Hero's lap.

"Try to finish it. I'll fix us something to eat."

Hero considered the remaining blanks until Mrs. Roth returned carrying a tray with two rippled green glasses of iced tea and a china plate heaped with wedges of cinnamon toast. They ate silently for a few minutes, looking at the puzzle. Hero licked her fingers. She hadn't had cinnamon toast in a long time. The crunchy sweetness reminded her of the elaborate tea parties she and Beatrice used to organize underneath the kitchen table when they were little.

"Well, I suppose we'll have to throw in the towel," Mrs. Roth said eventually. "I've grown too attached to these crosswords anyway. It's an 'old lady' habit, I'm afraid. I never used to bother with them. But now I find it gratifying to solve their little mysteries."

Hero nodded. "I read somewhere that it's supposed to be good for old people to do crossword puzzles. It'll keep you from getting senile."

Mrs. Roth smiled. "That certainly is an advantage."

She collected the dishes and carried them into the house, her voice echoing from somewhere inside. "Do you know who used to do the crosswords with me?

Arthur Murphy's wife, Eleanor. Did you have a chance to tell your classmates you're living in the Murphy diamond house?"

"Not exactly," Hero answered. "They were more interested to find out that one of the kids in the class has a dog named Hero."

Mrs. Roth appeared at the door, frowning. "Oh, heavens. What an unfortunate coincidence." She sat down next to Hero. "But you know, people always choose the best names for their dogs. No one names a dog Miriam, I can assure you."

Hero laughed. "No, I guess not. Anyway, tell me about the diamond."

Mrs. Roth leaned her head against the wood post. She gazed across the garden at the weathered gray shingles of the Netherfields' house.

"The diamond," she said. "Well, let's see. It was very large, almost the size of a walnut. Seventeen carats is enormous for a diamond, did you know that? It was yellowish, and not a particularly good cut, but that's because it was so old. An antique. I only saw it once, actually. It was part of a necklace, a very beautiful jeweled necklace that had been in Eleanor's family for centuries."

Hero cupped her hand, trying to picture a diamond

big enough to fill her palm. Even the diamond rings of millionaires and movie stars weren't that big. They certainly weren't that old. "Centuries?" she asked.

"Isn't that remarkable? Her family was English, as I told you, and this was an heirloom piece that Eleanor had inherited from a reclusive aunt on the Vere side. That was her maiden name—Vere."

Hero nodded impatiently. "So what happened to the diamond?"

"Well, the Murphys knew the necklace was so valuable they couldn't possibly afford the insurance. But they had the diamond itself appraised and got coverage for that. It was valued at almost a million dollars."

"Really?" Hero couldn't imagine owning anything worth so much money. "Did they put it in a safe or lock it up somewhere?"

Mrs. Roth smiled faintly. "That wasn't their style. They were very modest, private people. I don't think anyone but me knew about the necklace."

Hero clasped her hands around her knees. "But where is it now?"

Mrs. Roth sighed, still staring at the Netherfields' house. "One Saturday afternoon last year, while they were out, their house was broken into. They'd left the kitchen window open, and the thief supposedly climbed in. He didn't take much, just some cash from the kitchen drawer and the diamond. It was all very odd. Didn't take the necklace—just the diamond, removed it from the setting."

Hero turned to her, puzzled. "But I thought you said the necklace had jewels on it. Why didn't the thief steal the necklace?"

"That's just it. It didn't make sense. The necklace was an antique, worth a fortune. And the thief didn't take anything else of the Murphys' either, not the sterling silver, nor the electronics, not any of Eleanor's other jewelry. There were no fingerprints in the house except Arthur's and Eleanor's. There had been no other break-ins in the neighborhood. And the police found it strange that someone climbed through the window. I guess the back door was so old, it would have been easy to force open."

Hero rested her chin on her knees. "Did the police think they'd faked the whole thing?"

"Well, yes," Mrs. Roth said. "I suppose they did. As did the insurance company, of course. There were detectives prowling around for months. They even interviewed me." She looked at Hero more closely. "Are you sure you haven't heard any of this? It's common knowledge in town."

"My parents may have heard about it. But they

didn't say anything. Why would the Murphys do that? Just for the money?"

Mrs. Roth didn't answer. She smoothed her trousers, and Hero noticed how old her hands looked, the skin thin and white, a network of blue veins near the surface.

Hero asked again, "Why would they pretend the diamond was stolen?"

Mrs. Roth sighed. "They were very good friends of mine," she said finally.

Hero glanced at her. She fiddled with her shoelaces, waiting for a response. Why wasn't she answering? And then she thought she understood.

"You can tell me," Hero said slowly. "I won't tell anyone. There's nobody I could tell anyway."

"No?" Mrs. Roth turned to her, and her gaze was steady. "You're like me, then. There's nobody I can tell either. Eleanor was my closest friend. Isn't it strange? She's the one I'd most like to talk to about it, and she's gone." Her lips twitched. "There's a wonderful Emily Dickinson poem:

"I'm Nobody! Who are you?
Are you—Nobody—too?
Then there's a pair of us?
Don't tell! they'd advertise—you know!

How dreary—to be—Somebody!
How public—like a Frog—
To tell one's name—the livelong June—
To an admiring Bog!

"Do you know that one?"

Hero shook her head, smiling. "If anything gets quoted at our house, it's usually Shakespeare. But I like that."

"I do, too," Mrs. Roth said. She rested her head against the post again and looked out into the garden. "All right, then. Why would Arthur and Eleanor Murphy hide a diamond?"

Hero waited in the warm silence, eager for her to continue.

Finally she spoke again. "Two years ago, Eleanor became ill. It was cancer, very advanced; no one had any hope. But there was a treatment in Mexico, something experimental and very expensive. It wasn't covered by their health insurance. Arthur was certain it was the only thing that would save her."

Mrs. Roth seemed to be talking to herself now. "They couldn't afford it. Arthur wanted her to sell the necklace. Eleanor refused. She thought the necklace might have some sort of historical importance. The Vere family was descended from British nobility apparently."

"But if it was the only way to pay for the treatment she needed," Hero protested, "wouldn't she do it to save her own life?"

"I don't think she had any confidence she could be saved," Mrs. Roth said. "She wasn't a young woman. She seemed to accept it, that she was going to die."

"Really?" Hero couldn't imagine that. "She just gave up?"

"I don't think it was giving up. Her health declined noticeably about a year ago. It was a terrible thing to watch. She'd always been such a vibrant person, full of interests and curiosities. She became very weak. She couldn't read. We couldn't do the crosswords anymore. Arthur was just desperate. I'd never seen him like that." Mrs. Roth hesitated.

Hero sunk her chin into the hollow between her kneecaps, breathing the salty, grassy smell of her own skin. "So you think he did it? You think Mr. Murphy took the diamond himself?"

Mrs. Roth nodded. "I do, yes. I think the police were right. I think Arthur reported the diamond stolen for the insurance money. He thought it was the only way to save his wife."

"Did he get the money? Did he take her to Mexico?"

Mrs. Roth straightened, seeming to come out of her

reverie. "No, not in time. Because of the investigation, the insurance people delayed payment for months and months. Eleanor died last fall. So it was all for nothing. And Arthur couldn't bear to live here without her."

Hero stared at the ordinary shingled profile of her family's house. It looked so much like the other houses on the street, with its peaks and dormers, its aging shutters and bay windows. Who would have thought it had such a history?

"But why does anyone think he hid the diamond in the house?" she asked. "It would make more sense for him to take it with him, or give it to someone. Or at least to hide it someplace else."

"True," Mrs. Roth agreed. "But the investigation was very thorough. The Murphys didn't have many close friends, other than myself. And Arthur did finally receive the insurance settlement, which was nearly a million dollars. So if he'd turned up with the diamond, it would have been a serious matter legally."

Hero hugged her legs against her chest. What if the diamond were still in the house somewhere? Or buried in the yard? It could be tucked under a floorboard in the hallway, or pushed deep into the soft dirt beneath the azaleas.

"But Mr. Murphy moved out awhile ago, right?" Hero said suddenly. "And you said the whole town knows about the diamond. Someone might have already found it." She felt a stab of disappointment.

Mrs. Roth tilted her head, smiling at Hero. "Arthur did move out a few months ago. But the house has been locked up, empty. And the police searched it quite thoroughly. Wherever the diamond is, it isn't easy to find."

She rested her hand on Hero's shoulder. "You know, I think Arthur chose your family quite deliberately. He told me all about your father and his job at the Maxwell."

Hero looked at her curiously. She couldn't imagine what her father's job had to do with this. "Have you talked to Mr. Murphy? Since he left, I mean?"

Mrs. Roth shook her head. "I last spoke to him in June, when he decided to sell the house to your parents. He hasn't been in touch since. I think he's in Boston, but I'm not sure."

Hero glanced at her watch. "Oh!" she cried. "It's almost five o'clock. I have to go." She reached for her backpack reluctantly. "So you think the diamond's still there?"

Mrs. Roth stood slowly, using the porch column for

support. "Indeed I do. I have good reason to think so. Arthur—" she stopped. "You should go. I'll show you tomorrow."

"What?" Hero asked, unable to leave the porch. "What is it?"

Mrs. Roth smiled. "Tomorrow."

CHAPTER 5

Hero burst through the back door into the kitchen, where the rich, garlicky smell of tomato sauce filled the air. Her mother stood at the stove, a dripping spoon in one hand.

"Hero, where have you been? I was worried."

"Sorry." Hero unzipped her backpack and began sorting through it, dropping homework sheets on top of a stack of her mother's work papers in the middle of the kitchen table.

"Honey, those are invitations for an event at the Maxwell. Please don't make a mess. Why are you so late?"

"I stopped at Mrs. Roth's on the way home."

Her mother looked at her more closely. "Mrs. Roth's? Really? What were you doing over there?"

"Oh, nothing." Hero paused. "She was working on a crossword puzzle, and I helped her."

Hero's mother returned to her stirring, but her lips pursed skeptically. "How did school go today?" she asked.

Again, Hero hesitated. She wouldn't have minded her mother's sympathy, but often these things seemed to upset her parents more than they upset her. And then, in addition to worrying about her own problems, Hero had to worry about the two of them worrying about her problems, which was more exhausting than coping with the problems all by herself.

"School was okay," she said.

"Really?" her mother asked eagerly, searching Hero's face. "Everything went okay today?"

"Yeah, fine."

"Oh, honey, I'm so glad. The first day is always the hardest."

"Yeah, it is," Hero agreed.

She sank into a chair and crossed her arms over her homework, resting her head in the crook of her elbow. She could see the smooth ivory invitations her mother had been working on. They had ornate crimson script curling across them.

"Those are pretty," she said.

"Thank you. They're for the opening reception of that *Hamlet* exhibit your father's been talking about." Her mother glanced out the window. "Speak of the devil."

Hero heard the sound of her father's car in the driveway. A minute later he came through the door, scattering car keys and loose change right in front of her.

He ruffled her hair. "Hello, ladybird! How was the day?"

"Fine," Hero answered promptly, hoping to cut off further questions. She thought of Mrs. Roth's comment about her father's job. "Hey, Dad," she said. "Mrs. Roth told me the guy who sold us the house was really interested in what you do. You know, that you study Shakespeare and everything. She said it's why he sold the house to us."

"Mrs. Roth?" Her father looked at her blankly.

"The lady next door."

"Oh, right. Well, yes, that's true. It's an odd connection, isn't it? The wife's relationship to Edward de Vere, of all people."

Now it was Hero's turn to look blank. "What do you mean? Who's Edward de Vere?"

Her mother clucked in mock disapproval. "You girls never pay attention to your father. He told you about this when we went through the house after the closing."

"He did?" Hero had no recollection of any story about an Edward de Vere. But her father often digressed into long-winded literary lectures that she and Beatrice were in the habit of ignoring.

"Indeed I did," her father protested. "Edward de Vere, the seventeenth Earl of Oxford, the man who might be Shakespeare. Ring a bell?"

The Earl of Oxford did vaguely ring a bell. But what did he have to do with Shakespeare, or with the Murphys for that matter? "Tell me again," Hero said.

Her father pulled a chair away from the table and sat down next to her. He ran his hand over the short scruff of his beard and leaned forward intently. "Apparently, Arthur Murphy's late wife was a descendant of Edward de Vere, the Elizabethan courtier whom some believe is the real author of Shakespeare's plays and sonnets. The secret Shakespeare. There's no proof, of course, but there are some intriguing clues."

Hero looked at him, puzzled. "I don't get it. Why does anybody think Shakespeare didn't write his own plays?"

"Well, let's see. Three things, really. First, William Shakespeare was a humble merchant. He had no more than a grammar-school education and wasn't worldly or well-traveled as far as we know. Yet the plays depend on a vast knowledge of many subjects—literature, history, law, and geography—not to mention specific details of royal life."

"Couldn't he have learned about those things from books?" Hero asked.

"It's possible, but the point is, he wasn't an educated man. He was an ordinary businessman, without the library or other resources of a wealthier person. Then there's the second reason: When Shakespeare died, there were no obituaries or public homages paid to him. Think of that: a man now considered the greatest playwright of the English language and whose work was deservedly popular in its own time. He died quietly, praises unsung."

"What's the third reason?" Hero asked.

Her father tapped the edge of the table with his fingertips. "That's the most interesting of all. Shakespeare left behind no collection of books, no manuscripts of his plays or verses, no documents in his own handwriting that link him to the literature. It's very strange. Other Elizabethan playwrights and poets kept extensive libraries of their own and other writers' material. Actually, only six signatures in

Shakespeare's hand exist. They're quite primitive and show different spellings of his name."

"He couldn't even spell his own name?" Hero considered this. "Okay, so maybe he didn't write the plays."

Her mother laughed. "You were easy to convince. He's the greatest figure in English literature! Think what that would mean, if Shakespeare wasn't the author of those plays."

Hero shrugged. "But it wouldn't change the plays. I mean, they're still the same. Does it really matter who wrote them?"

Her father smiled at her. "'A rose by any other name would smell as sweet.'"

"Well, yeah. But, Dad, why do they think that other man, Vere, was the real author?"

Her father leaned back in his chair and loosened his tie. "Edward de Vere, the seventeenth Earl of Oxford. We call him Oxford, although you're right, his descendants go by the last name of Vere. Actually, the whole thing is hotly debated in my circles. Most academics still favor Shakespeare as the true author of the plays, barring proof to the contrary. But over the years, Oxford has emerged as a real possibility."

Hero could sense her father drifting into one of his lectures. She straightened her homework sheets impatiently and took a pencil out of her backpack. "But why?" she persisted. "What makes people think he's the secret Shakespeare?"

"Well, he has the right background," her father said. "The perfect background, really. He was clever, well educated, well traveled, a great favorite of Queen Elizabeth's, and frequently at court. Certain events of his life bear a fascinating resemblance to events in Shakespeare's plays. And recently, scholars discovered that Oxford's personal Bible was annotated—it had notes in the margins—and the marked passages correspond with important verses in Shakespeare's work."

"But did he write anything else? Could he spell his own name?" To Hero, that seemed a fairly basic test of a writer's skill.

Her father laughed. "Yes, indeed. Oxford left behind many literary documents. He was a well-known poet whose talent as a playwright was widely praised. But—and here's the other piece of the puzzle—historians have been unable to discover any plays published under his name. To some, that suggests he might have had a secret life, creating plays under a pseudonym: Shakespeare."

Hero looked at her father, balancing her pencil on her knuckle. "But why would he do that? Why wouldn't he want people to know he wrote those great plays?"

Her father stood, his chair scraping the floor as he pushed away from the table. "That's the key question, and no one's found a good answer to it. Some believe that it was beneath Oxford to publicly reveal himself as the author of the plays. They think that since he was a nobleman, his reputation would have suffered if his name were linked to the lowly pursuits of the theater. Playwriting was considered unworthy of the nobility."

"Do you think that?" Hero asked.

Her father paused. "Well, there was some prejudice against it, but it was fading during Queen Elizabeth's reign. And it's not as if he were royalty."

"So you don't think he's the real author?"

"To be honest, I don't know. There's a case to be made, absolutely. But I have to admit, I'm reluctant to give up the man from Stratford. The idea of a simple, unschooled merchant stringing together some of the most beautiful phrases in the English language . . . now that's inspiring." Her father's face creased in a smile. "Still, as Shakespeare himself would say, the play's the thing."

Hero glanced down at her math worksheet, with its orderly march of numbers followed by blanks: the promise of crisp solutions. "So nobody knows anything for sure," she said, disappointed. "What did Mr. Murphy say about it?"

"Well, naturally, his wife's family prefers to believe that Oxford—their ancestor Edward de Vere—is the true Shakespeare. And Murphy seemed quite convinced. But I asked if they'd ever come across any documents—papers, letters, anything—that supported it, and he didn't know of any. So I suspect it will remain a mystery."

Her father winked at her, tugging a strand of her hair. "I must say, Hero, I'm delighted by this sudden interest in Shakespeare. You know, we have plenty of books on sixteenth-century England in the study. You could do a little reading on it yourself if you'd like. I'd be happy to pull them out for you."

"Oh, that's okay," Hero said quickly. "I was just curious because of what Mrs. Roth said."

"Well, if you change your mind . . ." Her father started to leave the room but stopped at the door. "So, school went well today?"

Hero glanced up and saw her mother turn, too, both of them looking at her with expectant smiles, their faces reflecting exactly what they hoped she would say. It really was so much easier just to say it. "Yeah, fine. The teacher seems nice."

"There you go! You were worried for nothing." Her father thumped the door frame. "It's all in your attitude, Hero. That's the key."

Hero smiled at him. Her father was always so clueless about her real life. She felt a strange mixture of pity and gratitude. It was good to be home, in the bright, safe kitchen, with the smell of dinner filling the air and her parents bustling obliviously just a few feet away.

⋄ ⋄ ⋄

Later that night, as Hero and Beatrice crowded at the bathroom sink to brush their teeth, Beatrice demanded the real story.

"Okay, so what happened?" she asked impatiently. "Mom and Dad think you're finally well adjusted."

Hero laughed. "Oh, it was terrible. I got stuck showing a little kid where the first-grade classrooms were, so I was late. Then, when I had to say my name, it turned out there was some girl in my class with a dog named Hero, and of course she had to announce it to everybody."

"You're kidding."

"Nope. So, for the whole entire day, the other kids were whistling at me and making dog jokes."

Beatrice looked awed. "That's probably the worst first day you've ever had."

"Pretty much," Hero answered.

"And it's not like they're going to forget about the dog thing. Not any time soon."

"Probably not."

"Wow, that's rough." Beatrice flipped off the light switch and they drifted together into the hallway, silently assessing the damage.

"How was it for you today?" Hero asked. Part of her didn't want to know.

Beatrice shrugged. "It was okay. I mean, I get teased too, but nothing like that."

"You get teased?" Hero looked at her sister in amazement, feeling a small flicker of hope.

"Sure. Some of the boys were passing notes about me, and on the bus this afternoon, somebody behind me kept pulling on my hair."

"Oh, geez, Triss," Hero protested. "That's because they *like* you. Don't you see? That's their stupid way of getting your attention."

Beatrice paused. "Maybe," she said. "But it's still annoying."

Hero shook her head in disbelief. There were few things worse than having a beautiful, popular sister. It changed the way you looked at the world. And the way the world looked at you.

Beatrice stopped at the doorway of her bedroom. "You can sleep in here tonight if you want," she offered.

Hero changed into a T-shirt, grabbed a book, and padded barefoot into her sister's room. The large windows overlooked the backyard. She could see the moonlight streaming over the trees and bushes, making long, crazy shadows across the grass. Was there a diamond hidden out there somewhere? She looked at Beatrice, already settled under the covers. She wanted to tell her about the Murphys, but at the same time, she didn't. She wanted to keep the secret. To have something that belonged only to her.

CHAPTER 6

At school the next day, Hero decided her plan would be to attract as little attention as possible. She got to her classroom early, slid her notebooks into her desk, and steadily ignored the whispered dog comments that percolated from the back row. She found that if she avoided eye contact with Mrs. Vanderley, the teacher never called on her. Actually, she wondered if Mrs. Vanderley even remembered her name. By afternoon, Hero had decided to concentrate all her psychic energy on becoming part of the laminate wooden seat, solid yet invisible. If she could keep her name from being spoken out loud for a few days, maybe the other kids would forget the dog association.

With this as her goal, Hero slipped through the rest of the day as quietly as possible. She didn't talk to anyone. She didn't raise her hand in class. She sat by herself in the cafeteria and ate, quickly and unobtrusively, the tuna sandwich her mother had packed that morning. She couldn't entirely avoid the teasing. The boys standing behind her in the lunch line jostled one another and barked a few times. But, for the most part, they didn't bother Hero, which made her feel relieved. And alone.

⟡ ⟡ ⟡

When she got off the bus that afternoon, she forgot all about school in her eagerness to get to Mrs. Roth's. But as she was heading away from the corner, she heard frantic shouting.

"Ben! No! Give that back! Give it *back*! That's my hat!"

Hero stopped and turned. Aaron was racing around the street sign, yelling and sobbing, while two much bigger boys tossed his beloved Orioles cap back and forth. Hero immediately recognized them as two of the boys who had been waiting at the bus stop yesterday. The third boy was leaning against the street sign. She realized with a start that he was looking directly at her. He was tall, with blond hair falling over his forehead. To her amazement, he smiled.

She looked at him in confusion. Then, suddenly, she felt a surge of anger. She dropped her backpack on the pavement and strode back to the street corner. There was Aaron, running between the two other boys, beating them with his fists and trying futilely to grab the hat they waved just out of reach. "No, Ben! Give it back! It's mine!"

"Give him back his hat," Hero said loudly. She could feel her hands start to tremble. She clenched them at her sides.

The tall boy looked amused. The other two just stared at her. The one holding Aaron's hat had dark, curly hair, and something about him was familiar.

"What are you looking at?" the dark-haired boy demanded.

Hero could feel her cheeks grow hot. "Oh, I don't know," she said. "Just a couple of juvenile delinquents picking on a kid half their size."

The boy stepped toward her, and Hero deftly snatched the hat from his hand. She tossed it to Aaron, who clutched it to his chest and fled toward his front lawn, his skinny white legs flashing in the sun.

"Hey! What do you think you're doing?" The dark-haired boy yelled. He grabbed Hero's shoulder.

But the tall boy intervened. "Aren't you Beatrice Netherfield's sister?" he asked.

Hero shook free. All she wanted to do was get out of there.

"Yes," she mumbled. She turned and started walking away.

"You're Beatrice Netherfield's sister?" She heard the other two boys laugh incredulously.

"Whoa, you look *nothing* like her."

"What, are you adopted?"

Hero didn't turn back. She could see the picket fence surrounding Mrs. Roth's shimmering oasis of garden. She felt like a parched traveler in a desert. She began to run.

"Hey, Netherfield!" It was the tall boy. Hero kept running.

"Netherfield, wait up!"

She could hear him behind her. She stopped, her heart pounding.

"You forgot your backpack," he said, holding it out.

Hero took it and looped it carefully over her shoulder. "Thanks," she said coldly, turning away.

But, unbelievably, the boy fell in step beside her.

"I'm Danny Cordova," he continued, unfazed. "Don't listen to them." He gestured back toward the street corner. "They can be jerks."

"I thought they were your friends."

"They are. But sometimes they're jerks."

Hero frowned in annoyance. "Oh, and you're not.

That was really great, the way you stood up for Aaron back there."

Danny Cordova shrugged. "Listen, Aaron and Ben are brothers. They're always doing that kind of thing. I just stay out of it."

Hero flushed, embarrassed. Of course, *that* was who the dark-haired boy looked like: Aaron. How could she have been so stupid? She had meant to rescue Aaron from a neighborhood bully, but all she'd really done was gotten herself mixed up in a sibling quarrel.

"I didn't know," Hero muttered. Surely this would end the conversation. Hot and humiliated, she walked faster.

But Danny Cordova kept walking right beside her. "You live in the Murphy diamond house, don't you?"

"That's right," said Hero.

"Do you know the story?"

Hero nodded. "Yeah, I do."

They had reached Mrs. Roth's. Hero pushed open the gate, intending to say a curt good-bye. But to her astonishment, Danny Cordova followed her into the yard.

"Hi, Miriam," he called out.

Hero stared at him, speechless. Mrs. Roth rose from her seat on the porch, smiling warmly at both of them.

CHAPTER 7

"Well, Daniel! I haven't seen you in ages. How have you been?" Mrs. Roth took Danny's arm and beckoned Hero toward the porch.

Hero followed in utter bewilderment. What was going on? Had Mrs. Roth befriended every kid in the neighborhood? Did they all know about the diamond? Maybe she'd already discussed the Murphys with Danny and a dozen other people.

"You know each other?" Hero asked glumly as they all sat down on the steps.

"Daniel's father is the chief of police," Mrs. Roth replied. "We saw quite a lot of each other during the Murphy investigation. And I had the prudence to hire Daniel to do a little yard work for me last year."

"You did?" Hero found it hard to believe that anyone had ever done yard work at Mrs. Roth's.

"Just some weeding and planting," Danny interjected, seeing Hero's doubtful look.

"Oh, he was a great help," Mrs. Roth added, her voice warm. "Those tiger lilies over there are his doing, and my beautiful tulips last spring. I can't manage bulbs anymore. Would you two like something to eat? Cinnamon toast, Hero?"

"That'd be great," Danny answered. Hero nodded.

Mrs. Roth disappeared through the screen door, and they could hear her clattering in the kitchen. Hero shifted uncomfortably on the step. She wanted to be talking about the diamond with Mrs. Roth, not sitting here next to some boy she didn't know, whose best friends had just made fun of her.

"Hero? That's your name?" Danny raised his eyebrows.

"Yeah." Hero focused her attention on one of her shoelaces.

"That's kind of a strange name."

"It seems to be popular for pets."

Danny laughed. "I bet."

Mrs. Roth returned with their cinnamon toast, neat triangles scattered on a floral plate. She sat down between them, balancing the plate on her knees.

"Her name is from Shakespeare, you know," she said to Danny. "*Much Ado About Nothing.* Some of the less enlightened members of Hero's class have found it too distinctive to forego teasing her about it." She turned to Hero. "How did you fare today?"

Hero glanced at Danny, hesitating. She certainly didn't feel like discussing school in front of him. But Danny had the same look of easygoing interest.

"Somebody giving you a hard time?" he asked.

Hero tried to sound casual. "Sort of."

Mrs. Roth shook her head sympathetically. "Don't pay any attention, Hero. People can be quite unforgiving of anything that's the least bit different. But they'll come around."

Hero thought this sounded absurdly optimistic, but she remained quiet. Danny finished his cinnamon toast and brushed his hands on his jeans.

"My dad always says, some people will treat you badly and you can't help that. But how you handle it, and how it makes you feel, that's up to you."

"Exactly," said Mrs. Roth. "I knew your father and I would find one thing to agree on." She smiled conspiratorially at Hero. "Mr. Cordova and I didn't exactly see eye to eye during the Murphy investigation."

Danny stretched, looking across the garden to the Netherfields' house. "So, Miriam, did Mr. Murphy ever try to get in touch with you again? After he sold the house?"

Hero's heart sank. Mrs. Roth must have told him all about the Murphys.

But Mrs. Roth said simply, "No, he didn't. I think he may be in Boston."

Danny stepped down into the garden, idly yanking weeds. "My dad thinks the diamond might still be in the house. Somewhere. He's betting Mr. Murphy will try to contact you. You know, to get it back."

Mrs. Roth brushed the crumbs from her lap and stood. "Well, I would be happy to hear from him, but I really don't expect to. And I'm sure your father understands that I probably won't let the police know if I do."

Danny continued to pull fistfuls of weeds, piling them next to the walk. He flashed his wide, easy grin. "Don't worry. He's not expecting you to cooperate. He never expects me to cooperate either."

Mrs. Roth smiled back at him as she carried the empty plate into the house. Hero was left on the steps, not knowing what to think. On the one hand, at least the story of the Murphy diamond didn't seem likely to be passed around the bus stop the next morning. On the other hand, how could she talk to Mrs. Roth about anything important with Danny Cordova sitting two feet away?

When Mrs. Roth came back to the porch, Hero got up reluctantly. "I should go," she said. "I have tons of homework. My mom was worried when I got home so late yesterday."

Mrs. Roth's brow furrowed. "Oh, Hero. I was hoping—" she stopped. "I thought we could work on the crossword. But maybe tomorrow."

Danny stood up, wiping gray smears of dirt on his shorts. "I have to go, too," he said. He gathered the clump of weeds and tossed them into the bin at the side of the house.

"Thank you, Daniel," Mrs. Roth said. "I hope you'll stop by again soon."

"Bye, Miriam," he called.

He and Hero walked together toward the gate. At the street they turned in opposite directions.

"See you, Netherfield," he said over his shoulder.

"Bye," Hero answered quickly, heading for her driveway.

⋄ ⋄ ⋄

As soon as she reached the side door, it swung open. Beatrice grabbed her arm, pulling her into the kitchen.

"I can't believe you!" she squealed. "What were you doing walking home with Danny Cordova?"

"What do you mean?" Hero demanded, shaking free. "I wasn't walking home with him."

"Danny Cordova! Don't you know who he is? He's the hottest guy in the eighth grade."

Their mother looked at Hero questioningly as Beatrice ran to the window. "Were you at Mrs. Roth's again?" she asked.

"Yes," said Hero, "but I didn't stay long."

"Look, Mom," Beatrice continued. "Isn't he cute?"

"Well, I can only see the back of his head," Hero's mother remarked drily, "but I'm sure he's a nice-looking boy."

"He is." Beatrice sounded reverent. "He's cool, too. Doesn't care what anybody thinks of him."

"How do you know that?" Hero asked. "Geez, Triss, it's the second day of school! How do you know so much about him?"

Beatrice shrugged. "Everybody talks about him. He got suspended last year, and I guess it was kind of embarrassing because his dad's a cop."

Their mother raised her eyebrows.

"What did he get suspended for?" Hero asked.

"I don't know," said Beatrice. "Not drugs or anything. Something with a teacher."

"Well," their mother commented, "his reputation certainly precedes him. Tell me something, Beatrice.

Why is a boy more interesting to you and your friends if he has some kind of troubling background? I don't understand that."

Beatrice laughed. "Oh, come on, Mom, that doesn't make him *more* interesting. It just makes him interesting."

They all watched Danny's tall frame disappear down the street.

"What were you doing with him, Hero?" Beatrice asked again.

"Nothing," Hero said. "He asked if I was your sister, and—"

"He did?" Beatrice sounded pleased.

"Yeah, and then it turns out he knows Mrs. Roth. He used to do yard work for her."

Beatrice looked thoughtful. "Maybe I should start hanging out over there."

Hero laughed. "Yeah, it's a great place to meet guys."

Beatrice began to spread her homework on the table. "We'll probably never see him again."

"Probably not around here," Hero agreed. "But you'll see him at school."

Beatrice shook her head, cheerfully resigned. "Not alone like that," she said. "He's always with his friends."

Hero rummaged through her backpack for her Social Studies book, thinking about the strange afternoon. First the ridiculous mix-up with Aaron and his brother, then a wasted hour at Mrs. Roth's with some strange boy who, as it turned out, probably *was* a juvenile delinquent. The one thing that had carried her through the school day was the thought of hearing more about the Murphy diamond. But she'd found out nothing else about it, not even where to begin looking.

CHAPTER 8

As the bus approached the street corner the next afternoon, dark gray clouds massed overhead, and the first large drops of rain speckled the pavement. Hero searched the bus stop for any sign of Danny Cordova and his friends, but the corner was deserted. She felt a rush of relief, and then, though she wasn't sure why, a vague twinge of disappointment.

Aaron, who had been treating her like a returning war hero since the hat incident, commented suspiciously, "They're just laying low for a while. My mom really yelled at Ben yesterday."

"You could have told me he was your brother, you know," Hero said. "Then I wouldn't have felt so dumb afterward."

"He's not really my brother," Aaron answered. "He's, like, a stepbrother."

"He is? You mean you have different dads or something?"

"No, but he's *like* a stepbrother. He's always mean to me."

Hero tried not to smile. "You'd better run, Aaron. It looks like it's going to pour."

The words were barely out of her mouth when they heard a rumble of thunder. The rain fell in torrents, flooding the sidewalk. Hero held her backpack over her head and dashed down the street. By the time she reached Mrs. Roth's, her sneakers were soaked and squelching, and wet strands of hair stuck to her cheeks. She scampered over the puddled walkway to the porch, where Mrs. Roth held open the front door and motioned her inside.

Hero ran into the house, shaking her hair away from her face. Gingerly, she leaned her sodden backpack against the door.

"My goodness! You're wet to the bone," Mrs. Roth exclaimed. "Let me get you a towel."

Hero looked around. The inside of the house was not so different from the outside: shabby, cluttered, interesting. There were books everywhere, spilling out of the dark bookcases in the living room, stacked high on the dining-room table, even heaped on the piano in the corner. There were also flowers—marigolds, snapdragons, roses—stuffed haphazardly in odd-looking containers all over the room. A gleaming, ornately carved staircase curved away from Hero, and an old glass milk bottle filled with tiger lilies perched on the bottom step. On the wall straight ahead, a cluster of photographs hung next to a faded map of Australia and two large gilt-framed oil paintings of the ocean.

Mrs. Roth appeared with a thick blue towel in her outstretched hand. Hero buried her face in it. It smelled sweet, like detergent, and musty at the same time, as if it had been in the closet awhile. When she finished rubbing herself dry, she peeled off her shoes and socks and followed Mrs. Roth into the kitchen. A wreckage of bowls and baking supplies littered the countertop.

"I've made muffins," Mrs. Roth explained. "Blueberry, just put them in. Tea?" She filled the kettle and began pulling her china cups and saucers from the cupboard. "What a heavy rain! I love summer storms. They make the house feel so cozy."

Hero nodded. "My mom says that when it rains you never feel like you should be anywhere but home." She sat down at the table and looked through the window at the rain-drenched garden. "Hey, I asked my dad about Mr. Murphy. He said the reason Mr. Murphy was so interested in his job at the

Maxwell was because of Mrs. Murphy. She was descended from some Englishman who might be the real Shakespeare." She told the rest of the story, trying to remember all the details, looping back to correct herself, her words tumbling over one another. As Mrs. Roth listened, her eyes widened, and finally she slid into a chair and rested her chin in one palm. The teakettle whistled untended.

"Well, isn't that astonishing," she said when Hero finished. "I had no idea." She shook her head slowly. "Eleanor said the Veres were English nobility, but she never mentioned Shakespeare. If it's true—well, does your father really think it could be true?"

"He's not sure," Hero answered. "He says there's no proof. No one's been able to explain why Edward de Vere would try so hard to keep it a secret that he wrote the plays."

"Well, that *is* curious, isn't it?" Mrs. Roth agreed.

She poured their tea. Hero held the cup with both hands and lowered her face into the warm vapor. "You were going to show me something, remember?" she said. "The other day?"

"Of course I remember. I didn't want to bring it up in front of Daniel." Mrs. Roth sounded almost apologetic. "He's a dear, and I don't like deceiving him. But he *is* the son of the police chief. I'd rather not put him in the position of having to lie to his father. Or of having to tell his father the truth, for that matter."

So she hadn't told him anything after all. Hero smiled at her, feeling a warm swell of gladness that something remained a secret. "Yeah," she agreed. "Who knows if you can trust him?"

"Oh, I trust Daniel," Mrs. Roth said decisively. "I'm a notoriously good judge of character. But I'm not sure it's wise to trust him with information about the diamond. More for his sake than for ours."

Hero felt like asking Mrs. Roth if she knew about Danny Cordova's suspension last year. How trustworthy was a kid who'd been thrown out of school? But instead she changed the subject.

"What about his dad? His dad seems to think the diamond's still somewhere at our house, too."

"Yes. But he doesn't have as good a reason as I do." Mrs. Roth pushed back her chair and left the room. When she returned she held a small cardboard box in her hands.

"The day after Arthur Murphy decided to sell the house to your parents, he brought this to me. It was the last time I saw him." She lifted the flap of the box and gently tilted it over the table. There was a rustle of tissue paper, then a musical clinking sound. Hero caught her breath.

There in front of her was a glittering coil of gold, a heavy chain gleaming with pearls and rubies. An empty pendant dangled from the middle.

CHAPTER 9

"Oh!" cried Hero. "The necklace!"

She lifted it, still unable to breathe, and felt its cool weight settle in the furrows of her palm. It amazed her that something so old and fragile could seem so imposing. She was almost afraid to touch it. The rubies and pearls caught the light. The gold still glistened gamely.

"It's beautiful," Hero whispered.

"Yes, isn't it?" Mrs. Roth took the necklace and spread it on the table between them.

Hero saw that the chain had small, shimmering gold beads alternating with lustrous white pearls. Blood-red rubies set in gold brackets studded the length of the chain at regular intervals. The ornate golden pendant hung at the bottom, bordered by rubies, with a teardrop-shaped pearl dangling at the base. It was forlornly empty.

"So this is where the diamond was?" Hero asked.

"Yes, there in the center. It was a pyramid cut, square at the base, rising to a point."

Hero turned the pendant in her hand, looking at the rubies. On the back, she saw something faint etched in the gold. "What's this design? It looks like a bird."

Mrs. Roth nodded. "It's faded. I can't really tell. But it looks like a bird holding a tree branch, doesn't it? Eleanor said that animal designs were quite common in the jewelry of the period."

Hero kept squinting at the back, holding it closer to the kitchen light. She touched the surface with her index finger. Suddenly she had an idea. "Can I have a piece of paper and a pencil?" she asked.

Mrs. Roth pulled out one of the kitchen drawers and handed her a notepad and a stubby, pockmarked pencil. Hero pressed the paper against the back of the pendant and rubbed the pencil across it in dark strokes until the design appeared. She looked at it closely. "Are these initials?"

Mrs. Roth squinted at the page. "I hadn't noticed that. Yes, it looks like letters, doesn't it? *A* something. What's the second one?"

Hero shook her head. "It's pretty worn down. Maybe an *E*?"

"Hmm, *AE*. Some Vere ancestor, I suppose."

Hero gently nudged the necklace into a circle again. "It's so small," she said. "It's almost like a choker."

"Yes. That must have been the style. Or their necks were smaller in those days."

Hero tried to imagine the necklace clasped around a woman's slender throat. "How old is it?" she asked.

"Well, sixteenth century, so almost five hundred years old. Eleanor thought that it dated from the mid-1500s."

"I've never touched anything that old before." Hero stroked it lightly, full of wonder.

"Nor have I," Mrs. Roth said, smiling at her.

"But why did Mr. Murphy give it to you? I mean, it's so old and valuable, and it had been in Mrs. Murphy's family for such a long time. Why did he leave it here with you?"

Mrs. Roth tilted the box again and reached inside. She pulled out a note card, creamy white with a navy monogram emblazoned across the front. "This was also in the package," she said, handing it to Hero.

Hero opened the note card. Inside, in bold cursive, it read:

Miriam,
Eleanor would have wanted you to have this.
You were a good friend to her.
—A.

Hero frowned, puzzled. "It's from Mr. Murphy?"

"Yes."

"Is he giving you the necklace to keep?"

Mrs. Roth looked away, her face shadowed. She didn't say anything. Hero waited, but the silence gathered in the kitchen, as heavy as the downpour outside the window.

At last Mrs. Roth spoke. "They had no one else. No . . . children, no other family to give it to. I think Arthur wanted me to have it because he knew it would mean something to me."

"But you can't wear the necklace without the diamond in it."

"No," Mrs. Roth said. "I don't think that was his intention."

"Then what?" Hero wondered. "Does he think you know where the diamond is? Does he expect you to find it?"

Mrs. Roth took the necklace from Hero and curled

it in her hand, closing her fingers over it. "Read the back of the card," she said.

Hero turned the note card over and read, printed neatly across the back:

Do not go gentle into that good night.
Rage, rage against the dying of the light.

"What does that mean?" she asked.

"Oh, my dear. For someone named after an illustrious literary character, you have an alarming ignorance of English literature."

"We don't even study English literature in school," Hero protested. "I don't think you do that till seventh grade."

Mrs. Roth shook her head in mock dismay. "Is that an excuse? It's from a poem by Dylan Thomas. It's about dying. About how to die, really."

Hero kept looking at the card. "I don't get it. Did Mr. Murphy write this on the back? Why?"

"Because it's quite like Eleanor, I think. He wanted to remind me of her. And perhaps it has something to do with the diamond."

"Like a clue?" Hero asked eagerly. She studied the verse more closely. "Is he trying to tell you where he hid it?"

Mrs. Roth sipped her tea. "Let's not get ahead of ourselves."

"But you said that he thinks you know where the diamond is. He wants you to find it."

"Actually, Hero, you said that." Mrs. Roth seemed tired. She rubbed her forehead. "I don't know what Arthur thinks or what he wants to happen. It was horrible for the two of them during those last few months. All that uproar about the diamond, badgered by the police and the insurance investigators. And the whole time, Eleanor was dying. Even after she was gone, people were still talking about the diamond, the Murphy diamond. How much it was worth. Where it might be hidden. Would he get away with it. The poor man's wife had died, and nobody would leave him alone. It was all very . . . disappointing."

Hero looked out at the rainy day. "But why would Mr. Murphy give you the necklace unless he wanted you to have the diamond, too?"

Mrs. Roth opened her hand and stared at the necklace, absently touching the chain. "I imagine that he simply wanted the necklace and the diamond to be in the same place, as they'd been for over four hundred years. I think he wanted to put things right."

Abruptly she placed the necklace back in the box, folding the cardboard flaps closed. She seemed subdued, though Hero couldn't figure out why. They sat in silence for a few minutes.

Finally Hero asked, "Should I go now? You seem kind of tired."

"I'm sorry," Mrs. Roth said. "I'm not being a very good hostess, am I? It's just that—" She hesitated. "I miss my friend."

Hero felt a pang of envy. She tried to remember the last time she'd had a friend she liked well enough to miss. Not Kate or Lindsey, certainly.

The buzzer rang in the quiet kitchen, and Mrs. Roth hurried to open the oven door. A rush of heat filled the room, full of the fruity smell of the muffins. She carried the tin to the table and rested it on a pot holder between them.

Hero dropped a hot muffin onto her plate and blew on it, watching the steam swirl in the air. She had so many questions she wanted to ask, but she wasn't sure if Mrs. Roth was still in the mood to answer them.

After a minute, she said, "If the diamond is at my house, why do you think the police didn't find it? They would know where to look better than we would."

"True," said Mrs. Roth. "And you should have seen the mess they made. The house looked as if it really *had* been burglarized, by the time they finished with it."

"But if they didn't find the diamond after all that, do you think it's still there?"

"Well, it's a quandary, isn't it? But we have several advantages over the police, my dear. For one thing, Eleanor and Arthur. I know how they thought. I know what they cared about. And for another, we have a clue." She slid the note card across the table.

Hero looked again at its crisp, dark letters. "Still . . . it must be in a really good hiding place."

"A good finding place," Mrs. Roth said quietly.

"What?" Hero asked, puzzled.

But Mrs. Roth only shook her head. She seemed distant and sad.

"Okay," Hero said, trying to make things normal again. "Let's look at what he wrote. Let's try to figure out what it means." She read aloud the script that looped generously over the paper: "Eleanor would have wanted you to have this. You were a good friend to her."

And, then, turning it over:

"Do not go gentle into that good night.
Rage, rage against the dying of the light.

"The dying of the light," Hero repeated. "What's that? Sunset? Nighttime?"

"Perhaps," said Mrs. Roth. "But the poet is talking about death."

"Okay. But what 'rages' against death? Doctors? Medicine?"

Mrs. Roth took another sip of tea. "Well, yes, literally, I suppose. But also love. Hope. Memory."

Hero shook her head in frustration. "That doesn't help. Those aren't places you can hide something."

"No, not really. Unless love meant a gift, something concrete. Like a book."

Hero leaned forward excitedly. "A book of poems? A book with this poem in it?"

"That would be tidy. But there weren't any books left in the house, were there? Everything went with Arthur when he moved away."

Hero sighed. She took a big bite of the muffin. The blueberries were so hot they burned her tongue. "Maybe I should start by looking everywhere the Murphys would have kept books. Where they would have kept a poetry book. There are lots of built-in bookcases at our house, and weird cupboards and things. Maybe a board is loose somewhere, or there's a hidden compartment."

Mrs. Roth looked unconvinced. "That sounds like something out of a detective story, doesn't it?"

"Well, the clue is out of a book. Maybe the hiding place is, too."

"It's a starting point, I suppose."

"I'll check the bookcases and the medicine cabinets," Hero decided. "But, the problem is, how am I going to do this without my whole family figuring out that I'm looking for something?"

"You'll just have to do your searching when they're not around."

Hero stared out the window gloomily. "They're never not around."

Mrs. Roth patted her arm. "Then you'll have to be clever and take advantage of unforeseen opportunities."

"I guess," Hero answered doubtfully.

Together they watched the rain streaming down the window. The storm seemed to be letting up, but the garden was soaked and shimmering. The flowers drooped on their stems, skimming the wet ground.

Mrs. Roth lifted the note card and studied it. "This poem is about facing death belligerently, not meekly succumbing to it. Eleanor definitely wasn't meek. She wasn't one to give in. But there's a difference between giving in to something and accepting it." She set the card on the table again. "Eleanor accepted that she was going to die, but I'm not sure Arthur ever did. Actually, this poem is more about Arthur than Eleanor."

"Do you think that's important?" Hero asked.

"I don't know. Yes, it's important, but it probably doesn't have anything to do with the diamond."

Hero finished her muffin. "It's stopped raining," she said. "I should go home now. But I'll try to start looking this weekend."

"Let me know how it goes," Mrs. Roth said. "Oh, wait a minute. This is for you."

She reached behind to the kitchen counter and picked up a thick green book. It was battered from use, the corners rounded and soft. She handed it to Hero.

"What is it?" Hero asked. She lifted the cover and read the delicate black print: *The Complete Works of William Shakespeare*.

"I know you must have dozens of copies at home because of your father," Mrs. Roth said. "But I thought perhaps you'd like one of your own. You shouldn't have to wait until seventh grade to read the inspiration for your wonderful name."

Hero hesitated. She thought of her father, how Shakespeare belonged only to him. She ruffled the thin pages, staring at the dense columns of type.

Mrs. Roth laughed at her. "My dear, it's not a

homework assignment. You don't have to read the whole book. The play is very short. You'll like it."

"Okay, thanks," Hero said reluctantly. "But if it's boring, I'm probably not going to finish it."

Mrs. Roth smiled. "Spoken like a true scholar of English literature."

Hero took the paper with the pencil rubbing of the pendant and slid it into the book. In the entryway, she pulled on her wet socks and shoes, heaving the damp strap of her backpack over her shoulder. "See you later," she called to Mrs. Roth.

"Good luck with the search," Mrs. Roth called back to her.

Hugging the book to her chest, Hero picked her way through the wet shrubbery and across the shining garden.

CHAPTER 10

The next morning, Hero lay in bed listening to the faint murmur of breakfast noises rising from the kitchen. She could hear the whir of the coffee grinder, her parents' muted conversation, the occasional rustle of newspaper pages. Saturday, she thought: the weekend. She burrowed happily into her pillow. What a relief to have the school week over, no gym classes or cafeteria lines or bus stops for a while. Finally, she could start looking for that diamond.

The green book was on her nightstand. Hero picked it up and opened it across her chest. The delicate pages crinkled under her fingers, and unfamiliar words jumped out at her. *Anon. Thither. Twain.* It was like reading a Spanish dictionary. After some searching, she found *Much Ado About Nothing*. There was her name in bold at the beginning. *Dramatis Personae;*

that's me, thought Hero. She took out the paper with the etching of the pendant on it.

Beatrice came to the doorway, yawning and pushing her hair away from her face. "Are you awake?"

"Yeah." Hero slid her feet over the edge of the bed.

"What's the book?"

"Oh, just something Mrs. Roth gave me." Hero put it back on her nightstand, tucking the pencil rubbing into her T-shirt pocket before Beatrice could see it. "*Much Ado About Nothing.*"

Beatrice laughed. "Does she know we have about twenty copies of it?"

Hero shrugged. "She wanted me to have my own."

"Are you really going to read it?"

"I don't know. Maybe."

"Bet you won't understand it."

Together they padded down the stairs into the warm yellow light of the kitchen. Their parents sat at the table, drinking coffee and trading sections of the newspaper.

"There they are," Hero's father said. "All right, ladies, what's the plan for today?"

"I'm going over to Kelly's," Beatrice replied.

"I don't have a plan," said Hero, thinking about the diamond.

"Good, sweetheart." Hero's mother squeezed her

arm. "You can come with your father and me to the National Gallery. Are you sure you don't want to come too, Beatrice?"

Hero winced. "Mom, I don't want to go to a museum. Not on the weekend."

"There's a Van Dyck exhibit," her mother coaxed.

Beatrice shook her head. "I'm going with Kelly and Sara to a movie."

"Now, Beatrice, Hero," their father protested, "one of the advantages of living in this area is how close we are to the city. Think of all those wonderful cultural opportunities."

"I'll go some other time," Beatrice said. "I promised Kelly I'd come over."

With Beatrice standing firm, both of Hero's parents turned to her. "We can visit the Library of Congress instead, Hero," her father suggested. "If you'd prefer."

"No, Dad, I'd rather just stay home." Hero tried to think of some explanation that would sway them. "It's a nice day," she said. "I kind of want to be outside. I could do some yard work."

Her parents exchanged a look. "That's a generous offer," her mother said wryly. "What's going on?"

"Nothing. Really. I just want to hang out here. Is that okay?"

Her mother rubbed her forehead, surveying the kitchen. "I guess we could all stay. There's certainly enough to keep us busy. I could finish unpacking those boxes, and we could weed the flower bed near the garage."

Hero envisioned the day slipping away from her, filled with errands and yard chores and her parents' constant companionship. She made a final, desperate gamble, trying to sound casual.

"Oh, Mom, you do that kind of stuff every weekend. And then it's Monday, and you complain that we didn't have time for anything fun. You and Dad should go to the museum. Really."

She tried to look indifferent as her mother thought about it. Then her father intervened. "I've been wanting to see that Van Dyck exhibit. Let's do it." He winked at Hero. "The girls need some time to themselves, apparently."

"Hero needs some time to herself," Beatrice corrected. "I'm hanging out with Kelly and Sara." She looked at Hero curiously, as though she too wanted an explanation.

"Are we having pancakes?" Hero asked, reaching for a juice glass in the cupboard.

"Yes indeed. I was just about to get them started." Her father scooted his chair back, and in the general commotion of breakfast, everyone seemed to forget about Hero's strange request to spend the day alone.

⋄ ⋄ ⋄

Nonetheless, it took them a very long time to leave. Beatrice lingered in the shower, tried on three different outfits, and then took forever to repaint her nails. Hero's parents dug out various maps and spread them over the table, plotting their route into the city. Hero watched them restlessly, doodling on the newspaper. She took the pencil rubbing out of her T-shirt. Shielding it with her palm, she found a blank corner of newspaper and started copying the bird from the back of the pendant. She was just beginning to draw the tree branch in its outstretched claw when her father touched her hand.

He looked at her drawing, frowning slightly. "Where did you see that?" he asked.

Hero felt a quick pulse of guilt. She swallowed nervously, crumpling the pencil rubbing in her fist and dropping her hand beneath the table. "What do you mean? I'm just fooling around."

"It's not a branch," he said. "It's a scepter." Deftly, he sketched over her picture, putting a crown on the head of the bird and turning the tree branch into a monarch's staff.

Hero stared at him. "How did you know what I was drawing?"

Her father looked at her strangely, then smiled suddenly. "You've been in the study after all, haven't you? That story about Shakespeare and the Earl of Oxford has got you all fired up. You've been looking through my books on British nobility!" He nudged Hero's mother, his face flushed with pride. "Look at your daughter. She's drawn the Pembroke falcon, the crest of Anne Boleyn."

CHAPTER 11

Hero's mother glanced at the sketch. "Really? Oh, yes, a falcon. I see it." She turned to Hero, eyebrows raised. "What's gotten into you, Hero? Is this something else you've been discussing at Mrs. Roth's?"

Hero couldn't think what to say. She could barely think at all. In her mind, she kept seeing the initials on the back of the pendant, tiny and faint on the gold. Not *AE*, *AB*, Anne Boleyn, the wife of Henry VIII. The one who was beheaded. One of the ones who was beheaded. Hero couldn't remember anything else about her. She felt a shiver of excitement. Was it possible that the necklace had once belonged to Anne Boleyn? Was it a queen's necklace? A queen's diamond?

She tightened her fist around the pencil rubbing and looked up at her parents, trying to make her face blank. "Well, I was talking to Mrs. Roth about, you know, Shakespeare, and then we just started talking about English history. I got kind of interested in Anne Boleyn." That should be enough to get her father going.

"I can certainly see why," her father said, beaming at her. "She's a fascinating character. Started out as the king's girlfriend, just another pretty courtier, but she was clever and strong-willed, determined to be queen. She got her wish—his marriage to Catherine of Aragon was annulled—but she ruled only a few years before Henry's eye wandered again. Her enemies plotted against her and had her executed."

"She was beheaded, wasn't she?" Hero asked.

"Yes, on Tower Green. Falsely accused of adultery. Five men, including her brother of all people, were tortured to provoke confessions. Like your namesake, Hero: 'Done to death by slanderous tongues.' At the end, when she was imprisoned and sentenced to die, she showed extraordinary courage. And of course she was the mother of Elizabeth I, the greatest ruler in English history. I have a couple of excellent books on the era. I'll take them out for you." Her father went eagerly to his study.

Hero's mother continued to look at her curiously. "Are you sure you don't want to come with us?" she asked. "Your father could tell you more about Anne Boleyn."

"No, Mom," Hero said with conviction. "I really just want to stay here."

Hero was beginning to abandon all hope that she'd ever have the house to herself, when—simultaneously—Kelly's mother drove up, calling for Beatrice, and her parents realized there was a docent tour of the Van Dyck exhibit at eleven o'clock. With barely a good-bye, everyone rushed off at once.

⋄ ⋄ ⋄

As Hero watched their car swing out of the driveway, she sighed with relief. She couldn't wait to tell Mrs. Roth about Anne Boleyn. She saw that her father had left a fat history book on the counter for her: *Tudor England.* She flipped through it, skimming the pictures until she discovered a stark portrait of Anne Boleyn: dark, serious eyes, black hair sweeping neatly away from her forehead. She looked proud and bold. Her face showed no hint of the terrible things that lay ahead of her.

Below the portrait, Hero found the image of the falcon. It looked exactly like the etching on the pendant, but now she could see the details. Eagerly she read the caption: "Crest of Anne Boleyn, Marquess of Pembroke. This title and its emblem were awarded to Anne Boleyn by the king in 1532, to placate her during the lengthy debate over the annulment of Henry's first marriage."

Hero could see that the bird was standing near a bunch of roses, gripping a scepter, just as her father had drawn it. Mrs. Roth would be so excited about this! She stuffed the book in her backpack for her next visit.

At last, a few hours of uninterrupted diamond hunting. Hero drifted through the still house. Where should she begin? The bookcases? Each one of the downstairs rooms had some kind of built-in cupboard or cabinet, with flowery carvings and scrollwork in the trim. Unfortunately, Hero's mother had been sufficiently organized in her unpacking to fill most of them already—with books, knickknacks, delicate pieces of crystal.

Hero was determined to be thorough. She kept reminding herself that the house had already been searched once by the police, and the diamond had been hidden well enough to escape their notice. A diamond so big wouldn't be easy to conceal. Maybe it was tucked under something or inside something, some kind of hole or hollow.

In the living room, Hero pulled stacks of books off the shelves and checked for loose boards. In the dining room, she slid her fingers along the inside edges of the corner china cupboard, trying not to bang the slender handles of her mother's teacups. She checked for knotholes, mouse holes, grooves in the wood, soft spots in the plaster. By the middle of the afternoon, she'd examined every nook in the downstairs rooms, and with rising frustration, scoured the upstairs medicine cabinets as well. She found nothing but a pen cap, a nickel, and a chipped orange button.

Tired and bored, Hero thudded down the back steps into the bright sunlight. She stood in the driveway, picking at the splinters under her fingernails and glancing around. What if the diamond wasn't in the house, after all? She was just considering the leafy borders of the backyard when she heard the low rumble and scrape of a skateboard. She looked up to see Danny Cordova standing at the end of her driveway.

"Hey, Netherfield," Danny called to her. With a quick pivot, he flipped the skateboard into the air and caught it under his arm.

"Hi," Hero answered, hoping it didn't sound like an invitation. She flinched as Danny started down the driveway.

"I was at Ben's," he told her, as if he expected her to be interested. When Hero said nothing, he added, "Ben and Aaron are fighting again. Maybe you should go down there and break it up."

Hero scowled at him, but his easy grin made it hard not to smile. Triss was right. There was something about him.

"So what are you doing?" he asked.

"Nothing." Hero scuffed her sneaker in the loose gravel. "Just hanging out. My parents are in D.C., and Beatrice is over at a friend's house."

Danny was watching her steadily. "You're looking for it, aren't you?" he said.

Hero flushed and shook her head. But then, unbelievably, she heard herself say, "Yes."

She had no idea why she said it. She didn't trust Danny. She didn't even know him. And she was trying so hard to keep the diamond a secret from her own family, the people she did know and trust. But it was something about the way he looked at her, the friendly interest in his eyes. It had been a long time since any kid had looked at her that way: smiling, curious, wanting to hear what she had to say. It hadn't happened all summer; it hadn't happened at school.

Hero realized that if she'd had a really good friend to talk to, she would have told the friend about the Murphy diamond. Instead, she told Danny Cordova. And because she told him, suddenly it seemed that he must be her friend. It was mixed up. Usually, you confided in someone because you trusted the person. But she was trusting someone because she'd confided in him.

She watched him, wondering what he'd say.

"I figured you were looking for it." Danny grinned with satisfaction. He sat on his skateboard, rolling it back and forth with his feet. "Miriam's helping you, right? She could've told me. I know she doesn't want to get me in trouble with my dad, but I wouldn't have said anything."

"Oh, please, don't," Hero said, sitting cross-legged on the driveway. "You can't say *anything* to anybody. Really."

"Hey, don't worry. I won't. I'd like to find it too. It's worth a ton of money, you know. A million dollars or something."

Hero rested her chin in her hands and gazed at the backyard, at the grass growing too long in the shade, the sprawling rhododendrons and azaleas, the thicket of weeds next to the garage.

"I looked all over the house," Hero said. "Everywhere. All the bookshelves, all the cupboards, any place he could have hidden it. But I didn't find anything. I think it must be out here."

Danny shook his head. "No way. You weren't around for the police search. My dad had four detectives on it. And they didn't find any place that was dug up. Plus, my dad figured it wouldn't be safe for Murphy to leave a diamond out here. A dog could get to it, or some kid in the neighborhood. After it was stolen, we used to sneak over here all the time to look."

"You searched the yard?" Hero asked. This was beginning to seem hopeless. Maybe the diamond really had been stolen, and Mr. Murphy, crazy in his old age, had sent them a mysterious clue that had nothing to do with it.

Danny stood up. "This is what we should do," he said decisively. "We should look at the police report."

"Oh, sure," Hero joined in. "We'll just ask for a copy. No one will suspect a thing."

"No. No. Come on. We'll go down to the station."

Hero stared at him. "What do you mean? Just walk in there and request the Murphy file? Look, I don't know much about police work, but that stuff is probably, you know, confidential or something. Plus, they'll ask why we're interested. Plus, they'll never give it to a kid."

Danny grabbed her arm impatiently. "No, listen, we'll go right now. They're short staffed on weekends. My dad's there but he's on patrol, so we can hang out in his office. That's where the Murphy report is."

Hero frowned. "How do you know?"

"We used to talk about it, and one time he showed me. He still thinks it's an active case or something. He keeps it in his file cabinet."

"So you want to sneak in his office and look at it without anyone seeing us?"

"Yeah, exactly."

"How far away is it?"

"You got a bike? It's only a couple of miles. I can use my skateboard."

Hero hesitated. As a partner in detective work, Danny Cordova seemed a lot pushier than Mrs. Roth, and his ideas sounded more dangerous.

"What if we get caught?" she asked.

"Caught doing what?" Danny scoffed. "We're just going to visit my dad. Don't worry, they know me down there. And you'll be with me."

"Right," Hero nodded grimly. "And didn't you get suspended once?"

Danny looked at her in surprise. "Yeah, sure." He shrugged. "But that was a long time ago. And they don't suspend you for looking at police files."

"No, they probably arrest you," Hero muttered.

But she wheeled her bike out of the garage, and with the afternoon sun warm on their faces, they started down the street together.

CHAPTER 12

They rode down the street, past Mrs. Roth's yard with its burst of flowers, past Aaron's house, where someone was washing a car in the driveway. Hero pedaled through the river of soapsuds trying to keep up with Danny. At the corner, he turned sharply and stopped, waiting for her.

"You're pretty fast on that," she said, veering around him.

"Yeah, on the quiet streets. It's harder to keep up your speed when there's traffic."

"So how do we go? Grove?"

Grove Street was the main avenue from Hero's neighborhood into the center of town. It was a wide, long street with a steady stream of cars. The houses were bigger there, set back on deep lawns, with shrubs and fences shielding the yards from the road.

"Yeah, follow me," Danny told her.

Following someone on a skateboard, Hero discovered, could be a nerve-racking experience. Danny would sail ahead, then swerve and stop, often bumping into the curb when a car passed too close. As a result, Hero found herself pedaling furiously then slamming on her brakes. Once, a blue Jeep roared by and a girl leaned out the back window to yell, "Danny! Danny Cordova!"

Danny turned to wave, and Hero had to steer onto the sidewalk to avoid crashing into him.

"Let me ride in front," she said.

"But you don't know where you're going."

"Maybe not, but I won't get us both killed."

"Oh, come on. I was just waving. You worry too much."

Hero sighed. "Then watch where you're going."

"Hey, you're the one who almost ran into me. You watch where you're going."

Hero guided her bike into the street again. She glanced irritably at Danny. "Maybe this isn't a good idea."

"It's a great idea. And we're almost there, so quit complaining." Danny pushed off easily and coasted ahead, his slim frame shifting comfortably with the motion of the skateboard. Hero had no choice but to follow.

Finally they reached the end of Grove and turned on to Main. There was the police station, a squat brick building with brass letters on the side that read POLICE HEADQUARTERS.

"Headquarters, that's a joke," said Danny. "They've only got eight cops."

"Your dad is the head of everything?" asked Hero.

"Yeah, he runs the place."

"He must have been—" Hero paused. "Was he mad when you got suspended?"

Danny took her bike from her and leaned it against the wall in the parking lot. He clamped his skateboard under one arm.

"Not really," he said.

They walked through the double doors together, and Hero immediately felt her stomach clutch. She'd never been inside a police station before. They were standing in a tiny lobby. There was a bulletin board on one wall, covered in WANTED flyers that had bold letters with creepy photos. In front of them was a metal door with peeling paint and a large, sliding window. Through the window they could see a middle-aged woman with curly red hair typing at a computer. She smiled at Danny.

"Well, hi, hon. Did you come to see your dad? He's on patrol."

"He's still out? I thought he was coming back this afternoon."

"Not till later."

Danny hesitated, long enough that even Hero thought he looked like he was about to leave. Then he said, "Could we wait for him in his office?"

"Well, sure, of course you can. I'm just saying it could be awhile. Come on through."

The red-haired woman smiled again, looking curiously at Hero. She pressed a button on the edge of her desk. There was a buzzing noise, which made Hero jump, then a dull metallic thunk as the door unlocked. Danny pushed it open and Hero followed him inside.

The room they entered was large and plain, with a linoleum-tile floor, a few metal desks heaped with papers and file folders and, here and there, a stained coffee mug. At the back there was a separate office. Its half-glass wall overlooked the room. The red-haired woman returned to her typing, and Hero followed Danny into the rear office.

"This isn't exactly private," she whispered, as he shut the door. "She can see everything we're doing."

"I know," Danny said. "We have to be careful. Just sit here for a minute." He motioned toward a wooden chair against the wall. Hero sat stiffly, already feeling like a criminal.

"The file is over there in the cabinet," Danny said. "Bottom drawer. But we should sit here until she gets busy with something."

Hero nodded. "Are you sure she can't hear us?"

"No way. It's soundproof in here. This is the room they use for questioning."

They sat in silence for a few minutes, shooting quick glances at the secretary, who continued to type.

"So why did you get suspended?" Hero asked.

Danny looked at her. "Why do you care?"

"I don't," Hero said quickly. "Forget it."

He shrugged. "It's no big deal. I pushed a teacher."

"What do you mean, pushed her?"

"Him. I kind of shoved him. Not hard. But he said I hit him."

"Well, why did you do that?"

"He was picking on somebody. This girl he always picked on."

"Was she a friend of yours?" Hero tried to make sense of it. It was hard to imagine deliberately touching a teacher, much less pushing one.

"No, not a friend. Just some girl who showed up late for class, never had her homework. She never knew the answers when he called on her. So he'd dump all over her. And this time, he was yelling at her, and she was starting to cry, and he was leaning over her, in her face, saying, 'What's your problem? Are you lazy or are you stupid?' So I told him to stop. And he told me to sit down. And I kind of pushed him away from her . . . and then I got suspended."

Hero stared at him. "That's it? You got suspended for that?"

"Hitting a teacher," Danny said flatly.

"But, I mean . . ." Hero shook her head. "You shouldn't have been suspended for that."

Danny shrugged. "Whatever."

"Didn't you explain what happened? What happened with the girl?"

"It wouldn't have made any difference. They didn't like that girl. She was always getting into trouble."

"How long were you suspended for?"

"A week."

"Wow." Hero couldn't think of anything to say.

"It wasn't so bad," Danny said. He seemed amused by her reaction. "I just hung out and watched movies."

"Were your mom and dad mad at you?"

"Not really. My mom's not around. And my dad, he wasn't thrilled, but he never liked that teacher. He said he probably would've done the same thing."

Hero knew her own parents would have had more to say than that. There'd have been some relevant Shakespeare quote from her father at the very least.

"So where's your mom?" she asked.

Danny picked at a loose thread on his T-shirt. "She's not around," he said again. Then, reluctantly, "She's in California."

"Oh," Hero said. "How come? Are your parents divorced? Do you see her?"

Danny shook his head, still tugging on the thread. "I have her address and write to her sometimes. Every once in a while she calls. But I live with my dad."

He shifted in his chair to look at the secretary. Hero wanted to ask him more, but she was afraid he would unravel his entire shirt. The red-haired woman was facing the window, talking on the phone. She held it against her shoulder, using both hands to sort through the papers on the desk.

"She looks busy now," Danny said. "Let's find the Murphy file."

CHAPTER 13

Danny knelt by the file cabinet and with another glance at the secretary slid the drawer open. Hero could see that it was filled with files, packed with them. The manila folders bulged, wedged so tightly against one another that the tiny plastic labels along the top were impossible to read.

"Oh!" she exclaimed hopelessly. "How are we ever going to find it?"

Danny seemed at a loss. "I know it's here. But geez, if all these are unsolved cases, the police aren't doing such a good job."

"Have you ever seen your dad take it out? I mean, did he reach toward the back of the drawer, or the front, or where?"

"I don't remember. I think it was kind of in the middle." Danny sat back on his heels and started painstakingly pinching the labels apart, squinting at the names.

"Do you see something that says Murphy?"

"Uh, no. They're just labeled with numbers."

"Numbers? *Numbers?*" Hero crouched down next to him. "Are you kidding?"

Danny frowned. "What did you expect, Netherfield? Did you think it was going to say Murphy Diamond Mystery on it?"

"No," Hero snapped. "But maybe you should have thought of this before we came all the way down here. These are case numbers or something. There's no way we're going to figure out which—"

At that moment, they heard the doorknob turn. Hero scrambled backward in a panic, and Danny pushed the file drawer shut with such force it rattled the cabinet. But not before his father swung the door open.

"Danny? What do you think you're doing?"

Hero looked up miserably. Danny's father didn't resemble Danny at all: there was nothing friendly about him. Maybe it was the uniform, which was dark and frighteningly official. His hair was brown, and his face had none of Danny's lazy, easy openness. In fact, he looked almost mean. Or at least stern. Like a policeman.

Danny scrambled up from the floor. "Hey, Dad. Hey. We . . . we were waiting for you. Cheryl said we could wait in here, so we were just, you know, waiting."

Mr. Cordova looked at Hero. She tried to smile, but she couldn't stop staring at his gun.

"Hello," he said, not smiling. "Who are you?"

"Hero Netherfield." Her voice sounded like something between a squeak and a whisper.

"Carrie?"

Hero cleared her throat. Her heart was pounding. "No, Hero."

Mr. Cordova snorted, closing the door to the office. "What were you doing looking at those files?" he said sharply, this time to Danny.

Danny swallowed. "Well, see . . . we came down here . . . because, you know, Hero's doing that Civics project for sixth grade." Danny seemed to relax. He glanced at Hero, then flashed a quick smile at his father. "Remember? And she has to interview somebody who works for the town."

Mr. Cordova sat down behind his desk, studying them both. "I thought that project was in the spring."

Hero nodded. "It is," she heard herself say, and was amazed that her voice sounded steady and clear, no trace of a quaver. "But I wanted to start early. We just moved to town, so I don't know anybody, and Danny said you're a policeman—"

"Chief of police," Mr. Cordova said.

"Right, chief of police," Hero corrected herself. "And so I thought everybody must want to write about you." She could see Danny's smile getting wider. She took a deep breath. "So, anyway, I thought if I came early enough, then maybe nobody else would have asked you yet. And I was saying to Danny, you must not get many cases in such a small town, but he was just showing me how many files you have. It must be a lot of work."

Mr. Cordova leaned back in his chair and clasped his hands behind his head. He didn't say anything, just looked at her. The room was so quiet Hero could hear her heart thumping. She felt a pang of gratitude for her own vague, distracted father, her busy, cheerful mother.

Finally, Mr. Cordova said, "Where do you live?"

Hero hesitated. "On Oakdale."

"Whereabouts on Oakdale?"

Danny answered for her. "You know what's funny, Dad? They bought the Murphy house."

"Is that right?" Mr. Cordova leaned forward, still looking at Hero. "Well, Danny's probably told you about the Murphys."

"Yes," Hero said. "I mean, a little. I was thinking that for my report maybe I could interview you about that case. It must have been one of your more interesting ones."

Mr. Cordova shook his head. "No, not really. Pretty routine."

Hero glanced at Danny. "Routine?" she asked, puzzled. "But you never solved it, right?"

Mr. Cordova glanced at the file cabinet, and then his mouth relaxed, as if he were about to smile. "Oh, sure, we solved it. We just couldn't prove it. Not without the diamond. But I've been on this job twenty years, and I knew the minute I walked in that house, there hadn't been a break-in. No way was that a break-in."

Hero hesitated. "So you think they faked it? Do you think it's still there? The diamond?"

"I used to." Mr. Cordova seemed lost in thought. "But we went over the house and the yard about four different times, everything short of tearing up the floors and pulling down the ceilings. I think Murphy's got it with him, probably."

"You do?" Danny seemed as surprised by this as Hero was.

"Yes, I do." Mr. Cordova looked at them both in a way that suggested the conversation was coming to an end.

"It's not my case anymore," he added pensively, "but I'll tell you this much: There's nothing Murphy can do with that diamond. He can't sell it. He can't give it to anybody connected to him. He can't keep it anywhere the police might find it. If that diamond turns up on either of the principals, they're going to jail. Simple as that."

Hero looked at him in confusion. "What do you mean, the principal? What does she have to do with it?"

"The principals. The suspects."

"I thought Mr. Murphy was your only suspect, Dad," Danny interjected.

Mr. Cordova paused. Hero thought he looked reluctant, like he'd said more than he intended. "It's not my case anymore," he repeated. "Murphy's left town."

"But who's the other suspect?" Hero asked.

Mr. Cordova drummed his fingers on the desk. "You kids better skedaddle. I've got work to do here." He turned to Hero and said, not unkindly, "If you want to come down and ask me questions about my job, set something up with Cheryl, all right?"

"But, Dad," Danny protested. "You never said there was somebody else. Who's the other suspect?"

Mr. Cordova stood up abruptly. He swung open the door, gesturing to Hero and Danny. "Go on,

Danny," he said. "We'll talk about it later. I've got a meeting at four o'clock."

His son's crestfallen expression seemed to amuse him. He clapped his hand on Danny's shoulder as he pushed him through the door. "You know this already, Dan. You know her. It's Murphy's ex-wife."

Danny and Hero both looked at him blankly.

"Mr. Murphy has an ex-wife?" Hero asked.

Mr. Cordova turned to her. "She's your neighbor," he said. "Roth. Miriam Roth."

CHAPTER 14

By the time they pushed through the double doors of police headquarters, Hero could barely contain herself. She whirled on Danny in astonishment.

"Mrs. Roth was his *wife*? Did you know that?"

"No way." Danny shook his head in disbelief. "No way! I worked in her yard all last summer while the cops were there asking her questions. She never said anything like that. And my dad never told me either."

Danny held his skateboard against his side and crossed the parking lot. Hero steered her bike behind him. She thought about the afternoons at Mrs. Roth's house. All the conversations about the Murphys . . . and Mrs. Roth had never said a word. What did it mean?

"I can't believe she didn't tell me," she said to Danny, as he dropped the skateboard with a clatter onto the street.

He looked preoccupied. "Maybe she had a reason for not telling you."

Hero slid one leg over her bicycle seat, gripping the handlebars. "Like what?"

"Well . . ." Danny hesitated. "Maybe she's involved in it somehow. Maybe she knows where the diamond is. Maybe she's known the whole time."

Hero shook her head. "I can't believe that. I can't believe your dad's right about that."

Together they started back, Danny once again flying ahead; Hero, wary of cars, hugging close to the curb. She gave Danny a wide berth, anticipating his frequent stops and swerves. It was only when they turned onto Oakdale that she realized he was coming all the way home with her instead of turning off toward his own street.

As they reached Hero's house, she could see her parents' car in the driveway. Beatrice was sitting on the front stoop, and—Hero noticed unhappily—her friend Kelly was lounging next to her. Beatrice's friends tended to be almost as pretty as she was, but not nearly as nice. Kelly had long blond hair, white from the summer sun, and bright, dangling earrings. She was rolling up her shorts, assessing her tan line, when Hero and Danny came up the driveway.

"Hey, Danny." Kelly straightened, flashing what seemed to Hero an absurdly fake smile. She coiled her hair on top of her head with one hand. "What are you doing here?"

Danny flipped the skateboard up and caught it. He glanced at Hero. "I came over a while ago."

Kelly laughed. She stretched her long legs out in front of her. "What, were you looking for Beatrice and got stuck with her little sister?"

Hero felt her cheeks burn. She could see Beatrice was blushing too, elbowing Kelly in annoyance.

Danny didn't seem to know what to say. He looked from Hero to the two girls and then smiled his same easy smile. "Something like that."

Hero stared at him. *Something like that?* Furious, she turned and wheeled her bike to the garage.

"Netherfield," he called after her. Hero didn't look at him. She ran up the back steps to the house, the screen door slamming behind her.

Her mother was sitting at the kitchen table with several sheets of paper in front of her, comparing letterheads.

"There you are," she said. "Your father and I couldn't imagine where you went off to. Next time, leave a note, please." She held up two sheets of stationery. "Which do you like better, Buckingham or Bookman Old Style?"

"What's it for?" Hero asked. Her mother's guiding rule was that the style of the font had to match the nature of the business.

"Law firm."

Hero pointed. "That one. It seems snootier."

Her mother nodded. "You're right." She looked at Hero more closely. "What's the matter?"

"Nothing." Hero flopped in a chair and pretended to be interested in the stack of unopened mail, which turned out to be mostly advertisements.

"I see you got a lot of yard work done," her mother commented.

Hero grimaced. "Sorry. It was too hot."

"Mmm. And where were you all afternoon?"

"I rode my bike into town. Danny came over, and we went down to the police station to see his dad."

"Danny?"

"You know, Danny Cordova."

"Oh, that Danny. The legendary Danny Cordova."

Hero winced. "Stop, Mom."

Her mother smiled. "Okay." She kept looking at Hero. "But isn't he the boy who was suspended? I'm not sure I like the idea of you spending time with him."

"Oh, Mom," Hero protested. "It isn't like that. He's friends with Mrs. Roth, and his dad is the police chief." She felt vaguely pleased that her mother could imagine her getting into trouble, with Danny of all people. It seemed so beyond the realm of her ordinary life.

Her mother reached over and tucked Hero's hair behind her ear. "What's the matter?" she asked again.

"Nothing," Hero repeated. She rested her forehead on the cool tabletop, which smelled overwhelmingly of lemon furniture polish. She curled her arms around her head so her mother couldn't see her face.

"I'm just tired," she said. "It was a long bike ride."

Her mother put down her pen and ran her fingers through Hero's hair, stroking it back from her cheek. It was something she did whenever Hero or Beatrice seemed upset about something. The steady rhythm of her touch made Hero drowsy. She closed her eyes and felt her mother's fingernails slide against her scalp, pulling gently through her hair.

"Why did you name me Hero?" she asked. "I mean, I know it's from the play. But why did you choose Hero for me and Beatrice for Beatrice?"

Her mother's hand paused. "Well, you have to remember, you were just tiny, wrinkled newborns when we named you. It's not as if Beatrice seemed like a Beatrice, or you like a Hero. Nobody can look at a baby and know what kind of person she will grow into."

"So there wasn't a reason?"

Her mother kept stroking her hair. "I wouldn't say that. Your father and I loved both those names. If you would ever read the play, you'd understand. The two girls are cousins. Beatrice is bold, confident, full of fun."

"I know," Hero said. "Mrs. Roth said Beatrice is the stronger character."

"In the play, Beatrice is 'born in a merry hour.' That suits Beatrice, don't you think?"

Hero nodded glumly.

Her mother smoothed her hair back from her face. "And Hero is constant, brave, and true. Several men plot against her. She's engaged to be married, and they tell terrible lies about her, slandering her to her beloved Claudio. Claudio rejects her on their wedding day. He throws her aside at the altar. He accuses her of being wanton."

"Wanton?"

"Sleeping around," her mother explained. "But eventually the traitor's plot is revealed and Hero's honor is restored. The amazing thing is that she forgives Claudio. She's been horribly wronged by him, but she remains faithful and she forgives. She has a brave heart, but a gentle one."

Hero was silent, thinking.

"So," said her mother, "you see? Your names suit each of you well after all. Even though when you were tiny, wrinkled newborns, we had no way of knowing."

Hero couldn't believe that was how her parents saw her. Brave? Gentle? Faithful? It sounded like her mother was talking about somebody else. She felt flattered and bewildered at the same time. It wasn't at all how she saw herself.

She shifted her head under her mother's hand, her mind drifting back to Mrs. Roth and the diamond. Why wouldn't Mrs. Roth have told the truth about being Arthur Murphy's wife? What if Danny was right, that she was involved somehow? What if all of Mrs. Roth's "secrets" were really just lies? Maybe she'd hidden the diamond herself.

"What would you do if a friend lied to you?" she asked her mother.

Her mother was silent for a minute. "If I knew for sure that a friend had lied to me, I guess I'd try to figure out why."

"What if you couldn't figure it out, though? What if the only reason your friend would lie was a really bad one?"

Her mother lifted a handful of her hair, separating the tangles. "Well, if a friend lied about something that mattered to me, that was my business, then I guess I would ask her about it. It's hard to be friends with someone you don't trust."

Hero sighed. "But maybe if someone would lie to you, well, they weren't really your friend anyway."

"Maybe not," her mother answered. "But I wouldn't make a decision about that until I actually talked to the person."

Hero nodded, almost asleep. She would have to talk to Mrs. Roth. But it was all so strange. Mrs. Roth, Mr. Murphy's first wife? And living next door to him, best friends with his new wife? It didn't make any sense. She opened one eye. She could see the yellow shingles of Mrs. Roth's house through the kitchen window, almost blocked from view by the riot of flowers spilling over the fence.

CHAPTER 15

The next morning, Hero wandered morosely into the kitchen to prepare herself before confronting Mrs. Roth. She took a pint of chocolate ice cream from the freezer and set it on the countertop, fishing in the drawer for a spoon. Her parents sat at the kitchen table, separated by the stack of Sunday newspapers and the colorful litter of inserts.

"Hero," her mother protested, "you haven't even had breakfast yet."

"This is breakfast," Hero answered. She took a heaping spoonful of chocolaty ice cream and savored the cold sweetness on her tongue.

"At least put it in a bowl," her mother said.

"It's almost all gone anyway."

"Well, have a glass of orange juice with it."

Her father made a face. "With ice cream?"

"She needs something nutritious—"

Hero left them disagreeing and carried the carton of ice cream out the back door into the cool morning. She sat on the driveway, dangling her spoon over the asphalt and watching the chocolate drops stain a pattern between her sneakers. She concentrated on writing her initials. The neighborhood was silent, a Sunday morning stillness broken only by the shrill twittering of a bird somewhere overhead. Soon, Hero knew, people would be leaving for church, or tennis games, or shopping. But for now it was quiet.

Beyond the fence, she heard Mrs. Roth's door swing open and then her gentle footsteps on the porch. She looked up.

"Is that you, Hero?" Mrs. Roth crossed the garden.

"Yes." Hero stood up and walked over to the fence. She avoided the overgrown rosebush, looking for a spot not choked with branches.

"Well, why don't you come over?" Mrs. Roth asked, smiling. "I've been wondering what happened yesterday. How did you fare with your search?"

Hero paused. "I didn't find anything."

"And where did you look? Did you inspect all those lovely built-ins?" Mrs. Roth stepped carefully between the plantings to the fence. "Hero? What's wrong?"

Hero looked away. She took a deep breath. "Why didn't you tell me he was your husband? Why didn't you tell me you were Mr. Murphy's wife?"

Mrs. Roth stood still. Her face tightened. "Ex-wife," she said softly. "I am his ex-wife." She rested one hand on the fence, her mouth a thin line. "I didn't tell you because it doesn't matter."

"Doesn't matter?" Hero demanded. "Of course it matters! It changes everything."

She felt a surge of anger that surprised her. They had been in this together, she and Mrs. Roth, trying to find the diamond, helping each other, solving the puzzle. It had been their secret. But now it wasn't true. And wasn't the whole point of a secret that it *was* true, so true and private you couldn't tell anyone, or at least couldn't tell anyone except a friend you could trust?

Mrs. Roth gripped the fence. "It doesn't change anything." Hero saw her knuckles turn white. "Now listen to me, Hero. I'm sorry you had to learn that particular piece of information from someone other than myself. But it has no bearing whatsoever on anything I've told you about the Murphys or the diamond."

"You lied to me."

"I did not. If you had asked me about Arthur, I would have told you the truth."

"Oh, sure. Like I would have thought to ask that. Like anybody would! You don't even have the same last name. It's crazy. You live next door to your ex-husband and you're best friends with his new wife? Who'd believe that?"

"No one." Mrs. Roth looked away, dropping her hand from the fence. "Which is why I didn't tell you. I went back to my maiden name years ago, though I never quite gave up the 'Mrs.' At any rate, I was surprised when the police found out. But then, I suppose that's their job."

Hero shook her head bitterly. "It must've been a lot easier to fool me."

"I wasn't trying to fool anyone. Hero, stop this."

"What else haven't you told me? I bet you already know where the diamond is. It's not like you were so upset about your friend dying that you couldn't even think about it."

As soon as the words left her mouth, Hero regretted them. Something in Mrs. Roth's face changed, crumpling, closing. She stepped back from the fence.

"All right, Hero. That is quite enough. I'm sorry you believe that I lied to you. It was never my intent to deceive you."

Mrs. Roth turned away. She slowly retraced her steps through the thicket of shrubs and flowers, stiffly climbing the porch stairs. Her short silver hair capped her head like a soldier's helmet, glinting in the morning sun. She walked into the house, closing the door behind her.

Hero was left to stare at the jubilant tangle of the garden, dewy and sparkling in the morning light. She wondered why she suddenly felt so bad. She wasn't the one who'd lied. She hadn't done anything wrong.

She walked slowly back to the house. Hero ducked through the kitchen before her parents could waylay her and climbed the stairs to her room, flopping backward on the bed. The colorful glass bottles on the window seat caught her eye. Mrs. Roth would like those, too, Hero realized. She would fill them with her flowers.

She stared at the ceiling, studying the etching of roses on the old light fixture, all the while thinking about Mrs. Roth. It had been so exciting, to imagine the diamond, to consider its hiding place. It had been the one good thing about moving here, the only good thing. And now it seemed to be something else entirely: a lie, a scam, a hoax. Probably Danny's father was right. The diamond wasn't here anymore. Mr. Murphy and Mrs. Roth had taken care of that long ago.

Hero glanced at the green book on her nightstand. *Much Ado About Nothing.* That's the story of my life, she thought.

Beatrice leaned her head in the doorway. "Can I borrow your jean shorts?" she asked.

"No." Hero rolled on her side, looking out the window.

"What's the matter with you?"

"Nothing."

"Then let me borrow your shorts. Mine are in the laundry."

Hero sighed. "Okay. But leave me alone."

"What are you so mad about?"

"Nothing."

"Oh, come on. You've been in a bad mood since yesterday. What's the matter? Is it Danny?" Beatrice stripped, pulled on the shorts, and tried to see herself in the dresser mirror.

"No," Hero said firmly. "Danny's a jerk."

"No way. Danny's great. And he's totally into you."

Hero rolled over to see Beatrice's face, certain she was teasing. But Beatrice was absorbed in the contents of the dresser drawer, sorting through Hero's clothes for other possibilities.

"What about these black ones? Can I borrow these?"

"I guess. But you're wrong about Danny. He's a jerk, and if you see him at school, you can tell him that from me."

"Sure, like I'd ever do that." Beatrice snorted. She glanced up. "Hey, you can tell him yourself. He's standing in the driveway."

"What?" Hero bolted upright and looked out the window. There was Danny Cordova, skateboard in hand, walking toward the house. She groaned. "Oh, geez. What does he want now? Triss, you go. Tell him I'm not here."

"He'll never believe that. It's not even ten o'clock. Where would you be?"

"Tell him I'm at church."

Beatrice laughed loudly. "Really?"

"Just do it. I don't want to talk to him."

Beatrice shook her head and shoved Hero affectionately. "You're crazy, you know that? But okay, I'll tell him." She pulled on Hero's black shorts and a T-shirt, ran her fingers through her hair, then trotted down the stairs.

Hero heard her open the front door and call to Danny. She walked quickly to the landing, straining to hear what they were saying. She thought she heard Danny laugh. Beatrice wasn't closing the door to come back upstairs; she was standing outside, talking to him. Making him laugh. Hero fidgeted, leaning over the banister. She couldn't see anything, but there was no sign of the conversation ending, just the faint back-and-forth of their voices. What could they be talking about? Was he telling Beatrice about Mrs. Roth? About the diamond? In a flood of panic, Hero ran downstairs.

Danny and Beatrice were standing in the front yard. They both looked at her in surprise.

"How was church?" Danny asked, a slow grin lighting his face.

"Fine, thanks," Hero answered coldly.

"I didn't know you went to church." He was still smiling, waiting for her reaction.

Hero glared at him. "There's a lot you don't know about me."

He kept smiling. "Whatever."

Beatrice stretched. "I'm going to get some breakfast. See you later, Danny." Shooting a quick glance at Hero, she crossed the yard and went inside.

Danny pushed the skateboard with his foot, sending it careening across the driveway. It thudded softly against Mrs. Roth's fence. "So, are you going to talk to Miriam?"

Hero glared at him. "I already did."

"Did you ask about Mr. Murphy? Why she never told us she used to be married to him?"

Hero shrugged, looking at Mrs. Roth's house. She didn't answer.

"Oh, come on, Netherfield. What's up with you? You're acting like such a . . . girl."

In spite of herself, Hero almost smiled.

"What did she say?" Danny asked again.

Hero relented. "It didn't go very well. We kind of got in a fight."

Danny looked at her in amazement. "Really? I would've liked to see that. I can't picture Miriam yelling at anybody."

Hero sighed. "She didn't yell. It was mostly me."

"Oh, okay. That I can picture."

Hero frowned at him, but he only laughed. "I gotta go. Ben's waiting for me." He kicked the skateboard in front of him and pushed off, gliding to the end of the driveway. "See you later, Netherfield. Let me know if you find out anything."

Hero watched him turn neatly onto the street. Danny Cordova might be a jerk, but he certainly kept things interesting.

CHAPTER 16

When Hero walked into Mrs. Vanderley's classroom the next morning, she saw a knot of girls gathered at the desk behind hers. They looked at her when she came through the door, a deliberate appraising look, and immediately stopped talking. It was the group from the cafeteria: Kendra, Megan, some others. The popular kids. Hero was so startled by their attention that she almost forgot where to sit. Now what?

Kendra leaned forward as Hero unloaded her books from her backpack. "Hey. Didn't I see you riding your bike with Danny Cordova on Saturday afternoon?"

Hero didn't know what to say. She considered denying it, but that seemed likely to provoke more questions. She swallowed and said quickly, "Probably."

Megan smirked. "How do you know *him*?" The others were watching her closely, clearly waiting for something.

Hero hesitated. "He lives near me."

"But what were you doing with him?" Kendra asked. "Where were you going?"

"Oh, nowhere. We were just hanging out." Hero turned away nervously. She tried to busy herself with her homework, checking for her name at the top of each sheet.

"Hanging out?" Several of the girls giggled. "My sister says Danny Cordova wouldn't be caught dead hanging out with a sixth-grader," said Megan.

Kendra persisted. "You have a sister in eighth grade, right? Is he her boyfriend or something?"

Hero felt a flash of irritation. "No," she said over her shoulder.

"Is he your boyfriend, Hero?" someone asked. They were laughing openly now.

"No," Hero started to protest, but in her heart she knew it was hopeless.

"Ooo, he's Hero's boyfriend."

"Yeah, right."

"So what were you doing together?" Kendra asked again. "What was he doing with you?"

"Nothing," Hero repeated. She blinked back tears, her cheeks hot.

At that moment, Mrs. Vanderley walked in. "What's going on here?" she demanded. "Let me remind you that there will be a spelling test first thing this morning. If you've finished putting away your things, I suggest you review your vocabulary list. I want this room quiet. *Now.*"

The laughter subsided. Hero took out her spelling notebook and tried to focus on the long list of words. She wished she'd never met Danny Cordova. What had she been thinking, letting herself become friends with him. How could she have thought nobody would notice?

If the day stretched on interminably, the rest of the week only got worse. Soon Hero noticed that not just the girls but the boys were talking about her, laughing and then growing suddenly quiet when she passed by. She wasn't really surprised—that was how it worked. Something happened, something small like the dog joke, and they made fun of you. Then, because they'd made fun of you, you became a target. Anything you did was fair game.

There was no reason for it, not really. Or maybe there was. Maybe Kendra had a crush on Danny, or Megan's sister had a crush on Danny. And Hero had crossed some forbidden line, violated an unwritten law of the social order. She was the new kid with the weird name, not the type of girl who should be hanging around with the cutest boy in the eighth grade.

It wouldn't do any good to tell anyone. Beatrice had no experience with this kind of thing. Danny was the cause of the teasing, so it was better to leave him out of it. And Hero hadn't seen or talked to Mrs. Roth all week, not since their argument. She still had the heavy English history book in her backpack. She'd been lugging it to school every day, thinking about the initials on the pendant, wondering when—or if—she'd ever have a chance to tell Mrs. Roth about Anne Boleyn and the necklace.

⬦ ⬦ ⬦

By the time Hero boarded the bus to go home on Friday it seemed that the whole school knew about her and Danny Cordova, whatever there was to know. She leaned her forehead against the window and through the streaked glass watched the students flood out of the front doors of the school in their noisy, animated clusters. As they dispersed to buses and carpools and harried parents, Hero watched the fluid couplings and uncouplings of friends, the casual chatter and good-byes. It looked so easy, but in the end it was as mysterious as anything. As mysterious as the Murphy diamond, even.

Aaron interrupted her thoughts, squeezing into the seat behind her, clearly pleased with himself. "Hey! Guess what," he said eagerly. "I saw your name today! And you know what? I read it all by myself."

"You did?" Hero asked, not interested.

"You know how I knew it was your name?"

"No, how?"

"Because I see it all the time on that tag on your backpack. And then, when I saw the same letters, I knew it was your name. That's how."

"Oh," Hero answered. But seeing his flushed, proud expression, she tried again. "That's really good, that you can read."

"Yeah, it's really good. I'm one of the best readers in my whole class. The teacher says so. And I read your name, lots of times." He added solemnly, "You're famous."

Hero turned to look at him, suddenly paying closer attention. "What do you mean, famous?" she asked warily. "Where did you see my name?"

"In the boys' bathroom."

"The boys' bathroom? *My* name? Are you sure?"

"H-E-R-O. I told you, I read it myself."

"Oh." Hero shuddered. This was unbelievable. "Aaron, try to remember, what else did it say?"

Aaron thought for a minute. "I don't know," he said. "I couldn't read the rest. But it was your name, lots and lots of times. So you're famous."

Hero sighed. "That's not famous. Famous is a good thing," she said wearily. "When someone writes your name in the boys' bathroom, it's not a good thing."

"It's not?" Aaron looked surprised.

"No, never," said Hero.

The bus stopped at their corner, and they gathered their things and stepped down to the sidewalk. Hero felt overwhelmed by despair. What had the boys written about her? And how many kids had already seen it? Was that why everyone was laughing?

She thought about Anne Boleyn, about Hero from the play. She remembered what her father had said: "Done to death by slanderous tongues." Shivering, she hoisted her backpack over her shoulder. Without thinking, she headed straight toward the dingy white fence that bordered Mrs. Roth's garden.

CHAPTER 17

Mrs. Roth was sitting on the front stoop in a bright patch of sun, with the newspaper draped over her lap. Hero trudged up the path toward her, still feeling numb. She sank onto the porch steps, burying her face in her hands. Mrs. Roth said nothing, just shifted slightly to make room for her. Hero sat in silence, listening to the stillness of the garden, the breeze stirring the flowers, the faint hum of insects, the crackle of the paper. The smell of the flowers was thick and sweet and overpowering. It cleared her head of everything else. She understood suddenly why someone might love a garden.

"Six letters, beginning with *M*," Mrs. Roth said. "The clue is 'distinctly obvious.'"

Hero thought for a minute. "Don't know."

"Hmmm, I don't either. What about four letters, 'crowd protest'?"

"Riot?" Hero suggested.

"Oh, yes, of course. That makes it *m*-blank-*r*-blank-blank-blank for the first one."

Hero raised her head and looked at the grid, which was covered with Mrs. Roth's neat print. "How about 'morbid'?"

"Well, it would fit, but it has nothing to do with the clue. Let's see . . . aha! 'Marked.'"

"Oh, good." Hero scanned the remaining blanks, trying to concentrate. They traded the pen back and forth for a while, filling in what they could. Eventually Mrs. Roth folded the newspaper and set it aside.

"It's warm this afternoon," she said idly. "I keep expecting the weather to turn cooler, but perhaps we'll have summer for a bit longer." She stood, stretching, and pulled open the front door. "Lemonade?"

"Sure," Hero said. "That'd be great." She hesitated, then called through the screen, "I'm . . . sorry about the other day. I shouldn't have said those things to you. I don't know why I was so mad."

There was no response from inside. Hero waited nervously. Then Mrs. Roth returned with her tray, balancing the frosted glasses and the china plate of cinnamon toast. She rested it on the steps between them and sat down again, looking at Hero thoughtfully.

"I was surprised you were so angry," she said finally. "But then I realized you were angry because you consider me your friend. You felt I had betrayed your trust."

Hero looked away, embarrassed. "I guess I just thought you would have told me about being married to Mr. Murphy. Something important like that. It changes things."

Mrs. Roth sighed. "That's why I didn't tell you. Because it would have changed the story for you. It would have made you question my friendship with Eleanor, just as the police did." She rubbed her forehead, closing her eyes. "It's strange, isn't it? One small bit of information—a private relationship, something that happened a long time ago—and the whole story seems different. But why should that one fact be more important than anything else? Why should it make all the rest suspect?"

Hero shrugged. "I don't know. It's just hard to believe. People don't usually become best friends with their ex-husband's new wife. How did that happen?"

Mrs. Roth sipped her lemonade. After a minute, she spoke. "Arthur and I were married for nineteen years. There was no dramatic, terrible end to it. We didn't fight or come to hate each other. But something happened. . . ." She looked away. "And we couldn't go on together. So we divorced, but we remained close friends."

Hero didn't say anything. If they could stay friends, she didn't understand why they couldn't stay married. Being married didn't seem that hard; compared to putting up with your parents or your sister, for instance.

"When he married Eleanor," Mrs. Roth continued, "I was very happy for him. I liked her immensely. Is it strange that he would choose someone I liked so much? I don't think so. We had similar taste. At any rate, they moved here, and when I was ready to leave the city, they encouraged me to buy this house."

"Right next door to them?" Hero asked.

Mrs. Roth nodded. "That's odd, I suppose, on the face of it. It seems such a coincidence." She looked over at the Netherfields' house. "But really, there are no coincidences. Coincidences are just other people's choices, plans you don't know about."

Hero watched her lift her lemonade glass in both hands, turning it so it caught the sunlight. Mrs. Roth said, "I have no family except for Arthur. He always felt responsible for me. Through the years, Eleanor and I became close friends. When she died, both Arthur and I were devastated. We shared that. He couldn't bear to stay here. And I—well, I couldn't bear to leave."

They sat in silence for a while, and Hero felt the story hanging in the air between them.

"The Murphys didn't have any children? They had no one but you?" she asked.

Mrs. Roth looked away. Her face seemed different, full of shadows. "No. They didn't have children," she said slowly. "But Arthur and I had a child."

This was so unexpected that Hero almost dropped her glass of lemonade. "What?" she asked.

Mrs. Roth laced her fingers together, gazing steadily into the garden. "A daughter. My daughter, Anna."

Hero stared at her. "You never mentioned her before. Where is she?"

Mrs. Roth kept looking at the flowers. Her voice was barely louder than a whisper. "When we were married, Arthur and I found out we couldn't have children. It was something I desperately wanted. So we took a foster child, a little girl. She was so beautiful. Lovely blue eyes, the sweetest smile. She was four years old when she came to live with us. We adored her." Mrs. Roth sighed, folding and unfolding her hands. "But she was . . . troubled."

"What do you mean?"

"Well, now there would be a diagnosis for it. Depression probably. I'm not sure. As she got older, she had these startling mood swings. We didn't know anything. We thought it must be typical adolescence. But it was more than that. She ran away a week after her seventeenth birthday."

"She ran away? And you never found her?"

Mrs. Roth shook her head slightly. "She didn't want to be found. I know that now. But at the time, I couldn't stop looking. It was the only thing I cared about. And Arthur and I couldn't get past it. It was the end of our marriage."

Hero didn't know what to say. She touched Mrs. Roth's arm. "That's terrible."

Mrs. Roth turned to her then, and her face seemed creased with history and secrets. "Oh, my dear. There are no words for it."

"Did you ever find out where she went? Did she ever call you?"

"Years later, she sent me a postcard. It was from California, from Disneyland, actually. She was there on vacation. She said she'd gotten married, had a baby." Mrs. Roth sighed. "Isn't that remarkable? I might have been a grandmother to some little girl or boy."

"But couldn't you find her after that?" Hero asked.

"Well, I did think about hiring another private investigator. But, as I said, it was so clear that Anna didn't want to be found. I finally realized I had to respect that."

"Wow." Hero stared out at the garden, at its colorful, unkempt beauty. She'd never met anyone like Mrs. Roth, anyone who was as good at letting things be, accepting them in all their messiness and imperfection. But this was so sad. Hero wanted to help her somehow, to make her feel better. Suddenly she remembered the book in her backpack.

"Oh!" Hero said. "I have something to show you—about the necklace." She pulled out the book and paged through it, finding the image of the falcon. "Look at this," she said.

"Why, it's the bird from the pendant!" Mrs. Roth exclaimed. "How did you find it?"

"I was copying it from that pencil rubbing I made, and my dad saw the sketch, and he said it was Anne Boleyn's crest—"

"The wife of Henry VIII?" Mrs. Roth interrupted, staring at Hero. "The queen?"

"Yes!" Hero leaned forward, smiling. "The initials, remember? Not *AE; AB*."

Mrs. Roth gasped. "But that means—"

"I know," Hero said happily. "The necklace must have belonged to her!"

"Well, this is amazing." Mrs. Roth grabbed Hero's hand. "Oh, how I wish Eleanor could hear this! Her ancestors inherited a necklace from the queen of England." She paused. "But I wonder how that happened. Eleanor said the necklace came from her Vere family ancestors. How would Edward de Vere have gotten Anne Boleyn's necklace?"

Hero thumbed through the book. "I don't know. Were they related?"

"No, I'm sure not," Mrs. Roth said. "If there were a family relation to royalty—Anne Boleyn of all people—Eleanor would have known."

"Maybe they were friends? He was a nobleman, right?"

"It's possible. But it seems unlikely that she would give such a valuable necklace to a mere friend. I wonder what the connection was between them."

Hero thought for a minute. "I can ask my dad about it. He recognized the falcon. Maybe he'd have some idea." She continued turning the pages of the book. "Look," she said, sliding it across her lap so Mrs. Roth could see. "It says that a skilled swordsman came over from France for the execution. Anne Boleyn said, 'I have heard that the executioner is very good. And I have a little neck.'"

"That's right," Mrs. Roth said. "I remember that. A little neck. And it is a little necklace."

Hero thought of the small circle of pearls and rubies. Her eyes darted over the page. "Oh! Listen," she cried. "Here are Anne Boleyn's last words, right before she was beheaded on Tower Green:

"Good Christian people, I am come hither to die, for according to the law, and by the law I am judged to die, and therefore I will speak nothing against it. I am come hither to accuse no man, nor to speak anything of that, whereof I am accused and condemned to die, but I pray God save the king and send him long to reign over you, for a gentler nor more merciful prince was there never: and to me he was ever a good, a gentle and sovereign lord. And if any person will meddle of my cause, I require them to judge the best. And thus I take my leave of this world and of you all, and I heartily desire you all to pray for me. O Lord have mercy on me, to God I commend my soul."

Hero looked up. "It says here that she was only twenty-nine years old." She read the words again, to herself. "She was very brave, wasn't she?"

Mrs. Roth nodded. "Oh, yes. And honorable."

Hero bit her lip. "I mean, at the end it seems like she forgave all those people who lied about her. Even her husband, the king. And it was all his fault that she had to die." Hero frowned. "I wonder how she could forgive that."

"Well," Mrs. Roth said slowly, "I suppose we never know what we have the capacity to forgive until we're truly tested."

They were considering this in silence when they heard the familiar skid of a skateboard out on the street.

CHAPTER 18

As Danny came through the front gate, Hero felt a resurgence of the week's misery. She couldn't help glaring at him, thinking about everything that might be written on a metal stall in the boys' bathroom.

But Mrs. Roth called out warmly. "Hello, Daniel! How are you? Come join us."

Danny strode toward them, dropping the skateboard with a clatter on the walkway. He stretched out comfortably on the bottom step of the porch.

"Hey, Miriam," he said. "Did Netherfield tell you we tried to check the police file on the Murphys?"

Mrs. Roth looked at Hero in surprise.

Hero said reluctantly, "Danny knows about the diamond. He pretty much figured it out." She paused, racked with guilt. *But I didn't tell him about the necklace*, she wanted to say. *I didn't tell him anything we talked about*. She knew how she would have felt if Mrs. Roth had shared their secret. But Mrs. Roth only nodded at her, her blue eyes clear and kind.

"So, anyway," Hero continued, "Danny had the brilliant idea of sneaking into his dad's office to see the police report. Only guess what—we got caught."

Mrs. Roth turned to Danny. "Oh my. Whatever did you tell your father?"

"We made something up," Danny answered promptly. "About a school project. We said Netherfield needed to interview him. He went for it hook, line, and sinker."

Mrs. Roth shook her head. "You shouldn't lie to the people you care about," she said gently. "Especially if you think you might get away with it." She tilted her glass of lemonade so the ice clinked and settled. "That's why I never told you anything myself, Daniel, last summer when you worked on the garden. I didn't want you to have to lie to your father. Or to have to conceal something from him."

Danny rested one foot on his skateboard and pushed it back and forth over the uneven flagstones. "That's what I figured," he said. "But, you know, I wouldn't have told him. That diamond doesn't belong to the police."

Hero wondered if he was right about that. If the

diamond was stolen property, it probably did belong to the police, at least until the insurance company could claim it. She watched Danny swivel the skateboard with his heel. He looked up at Mrs. Roth.

"So where do you think it is? Really. If it's in the house, it's got to be in a good hiding place."

"A good finding place," Mrs. Roth corrected, then smiled. She turned to Hero. "What my daughter used to say about hide-and-seek. She was always looking for a good finding place."

Danny looked at her strangely. "What did you say?"

Hero turned to him. "I know, it's weird, isn't it? Mrs. Roth has a daughter, a girl she adopted when she was married to Mr. Murphy. She ran away a long time ago."

Danny looked at Mrs. Roth in surprise. "Really? You have a kid? How come you never said anything about her?"

"I suppose I think of her as part of that other life, my life with Arthur."

They sat in silence together. Hero thought about all the things that were lost: not just the diamond, but Anna as well as Mrs. Roth's old life as a wife and mother. She noticed that even Danny seemed preoccupied.

"What would you do with the diamond if you found it?" he asked suddenly.

Mrs. Roth smiled. "Put it back where it belongs. Look at it. Remember Eleanor."

Hero shrugged. "I never thought that far."

"Oh, come on," Danny protested. "It's worth almost a million dollars. What would you do with a ton of money like that?"

"Ah, the money," Mrs. Roth said teasingly. "What would I do with that kind of money? Travel, perhaps. I'd love to go to Australia. I've always wanted to visit the desert there."

"Me too," Hero said enthusiastically. "I'd travel, too. I'd love to go someplace really different. Any place. I'd get as far away from here as I could."

Mrs. Roth studied her. "More dog jokes?"

Hero shot a glance at Danny. "Sort of."

"Oh, yeah," Danny said. "I heard Aaron talking about it. You're famous."

Hero looked away. "Thanks to you," she muttered.

"Oh, come on, don't let them bug you. It doesn't mean anything. I'll get rid of it if you want me to."

Mrs. Roth looked at them in bewilderment. "What happened, Hero?"

Hero scuffed her sneakers on the edge of the step.

"One of the girls in my class saw me with Danny on Saturday, when we were going to the police station. When I got to school on Monday, she was asking me about it, and then everybody started making fun of me." She paused, embarrassed. "Some of the boys wrote things about me in the bathroom."

Mrs. Roth pursed her lips. "What kind of things?"

Hero twisted one of her shoelaces. "I don't know. But I can guess."

Danny touched her arm. When she turned to him, he said coaxingly, "Listen, I can get rid of it. Really. I'll do it tonight. The window on that bathroom doesn't latch. We used to sneak in there after school all the time to—" He stopped, grinning at Mrs. Roth. "Anyway, my dad has cans of black spray paint in the garage. The cops use it to get rid of graffiti. I'll cover up whatever they wrote."

Hero felt a flicker of hope, but Mrs. Roth shook her head firmly. "No, no. You mustn't do anything like that, Daniel. Breaking and entering, defacing public property. It's wrong. You're a policeman's son, for heaven's sake. What if you get caught?" She turned to Hero. "You should speak to your teacher, Hero. However deplorable, I'm sure this isn't the first time such a thing has happened."

Hero glanced at her doubtfully.

"Who's your teacher?" Danny asked.

"Mrs. Vanderley."

He looked skeptical.

Hero sighed, standing up. "I have homework."

"May I keep the book here?" Mrs. Roth asked, lifting *Tudor England* from the porch step. "I'd like to look at it."

"Sure," said Hero. "And I'll talk to my dad about"—she glanced at Danny—"you know, the other things."

"Good." Mrs. Roth patted her shoulder. "Don't worry, Hero. I know you've had a hard time, but you mustn't lose faith. Remember your namesake. 'Who can blot that name with any just reproach?' Think of Shakespeare. He puts everything in perspective. It will be all right."

Danny gave the skateboard a hard kick. "Yeah, it will," he said with conviction. He looked at Hero, and at that moment she recognized his father in his face. Beneath the easy smile and the laughing blue eyes there was something unyielding, a kind of determination. As she walked home, she shivered, dreading the thought of school on Monday.

CHAPTER 19

That night, after dinner, Hero found her father in his study, reading. "Dad, can I ask you something?"

He slid the book aside and turned to her. "Of course. What is it?"

"Well, I've been looking at that history book you gave me, and I just wondered, do you know of any connection between Edward de Vere and Anne Boleyn?"

Her father tilted back in his chair. "No. Why do you ask? Anne Boleyn was executed in 1536, and Edward de Vere was born later. Let's see. . . ." He reached for the bookshelf and pulled out a slim volume. "This is another one you should look at. It's a collection of papers about the theory that Edward de Vere was the real Shakespeare." He opened the book and flipped through it. "Here. Edward de Vere was born in 1550 or thereabouts. The dating from that era is notoriously inaccurate. But that's fourteen years after Anne Boleyn's death. I don't know of any link between those two." He handed the book to Hero. "The connection was with Queen Elizabeth."

Hero turned the pages. "What connection?" she asked. She found a portrait of Elizabeth I, with her red curls and white face, sitting stiffly in an elaborate jeweled gown.

"Well," her father began, clasping his hands behind his head. "It's unclear, actually. There's much speculation, even that he might have been her lover. But what's known is that, from the time he was small, de Vere—Oxford, as we call him—was a great favorite of Queen Elizabeth's. His father died and he was raised by one of her top advisors. When Oxford was an adult, Elizabeth gave him an allowance of a thousand pounds a year."

"A thousand pounds?" Hero asked. "That doesn't sound like a lot."

"Not in today's currency." Her father smiled. "But at the time, it was a small fortune, the equivalent of around $700,000 dollars now."

"Oh!" Hero said. "That is a lot. Why did she give him so much money?"

Her father ruffled his hair so that it puffed in a wiry cloud around his face. "The Oxford theorists believe that the allowance is another piece of the puzzle. That Elizabeth was paying him to write the plays but not take credit for them."

"To keep it a secret?"

"It's a theory. Again, it's intriguing, but there's no proof."

"But why would she care?" Hero asked. "Why would she care if Edward de Vere wrote the plays under his own name?"

Her father nodded. "Exactly. If there were some connection between Oxford and Elizabeth that meant the royal name would be besmirched by his ambitions as a playwright—but no one has ever uncovered that kind of connection." He reached out and tugged her ponytail. "It's fascinating, isn't it? Elizabethan history."

Hero had never thought so before. But she could see it now, what her father loved about Shakespeare, about that entire, mysterious time, with its pomp and majesty, secrets and betrayals. She nodded slowly, looking down at the portrait of Elizabeth and thinking again of poor Anne Boleyn, facing her death on Tower Green.

"Dad—" Hero hesitated.

"What is it, ladybird?"

"Anne Boleyn . . . they told those terrible lies about her. But I was reading what she said right before she died, and she didn't defend herself. She didn't say it wasn't true. Why?"

Her father rubbed one hand over his rough beard. "It wouldn't have made any difference. There was no escaping her fate at that point. The king wanted her gone, and remember, her enemies had tortured her own brother and four other men to get confessions. Those poor fellows were sentenced to be drawn and quartered."

"What's that?" Hero asked.

"Medieval torture. They tied each leg and arm of the victim to separate horses, and sent the four horses running in different directions. The person was literally torn apart."

"Ugh!" Hero cried, wincing. "Really?"

Her father looked sheepish suddenly. "Well, the king changed the sentence. They were beheaded just like Anne in the end. But your mother probably wouldn't appreciate my telling you all this. Don't repeat it, all right?"

"I won't," Hero promised. "But Dad," she persisted, "even if it wouldn't have changed anything, why wouldn't Anne Boleyn want people to know the truth?"

Her father ran his hands through his hair again, this time raking it smooth. "I remember her speech on Tower Green very well," he said thoughtfully. "The first time I read it, it gave me chills. It was elegant, but so full of courage. Don't you think people knew the truth from that speech, Hero? Sometimes the best way to defend one's honor is simply to behave honorably."

Hero was quiet for a minute. "Still?" she asked finally. "Even today?"

Her father smiled at her. "Even today." He gestured toward the book. "Have a look at that. See what you think about the Oxford theory."

⟡ ⟡ ⟡

Hero climbed the stairs, slowly turning the pages. The portrait of Edward de Vere showed a pale man with dark eyes. A frilly lace ruff framed his jaw, and a velvet cap angled jauntily over his forehead. The portrait of William Shakespeare was one that Hero had seen before: a balding sober-looking man with a broad, plain collar. Their faces gave away nothing. Who could tell which man was the true author of the plays? Shakespeare's secret was safe. Maybe it would always be safe.

"What are you looking at?" Beatrice asked, passing her in the hallway.

"Just a book Dad gave me." Hero closed it and tucked it under her arm. Beatrice followed her into her room. "So how's it going at school?" she asked.

Hero felt equally unprepared to lie or tell the truth. She lay on her bed and fiddled with a corner of the pillowcase. "Oh, you know."

"Are they still making fun of you?"

"Pretty much."

Beatrice picked up Hero's hairbrush and sat on the edge of the bed, brushing her hair. "You need a way in," she said.

Hero looked at her. "What do you mean?"

"You need a way in. Just one person. I know you think they either hate you or they like you, but that's not how it works. You just need one person to let you in, the right person, and then the rest is easy."

Hero snorted. "What do you know about it? You never have any problem fitting in. You're 'in' from the very first minute."

"No. No, I'm not." Beatrice put down the hairbrush. "I needed Kelly."

"Kelly!" Hero groaned. "She's so mean. Why are you even friends with her?"

Beatrice sighed. "She's my way in. It's not always someone you like, you know."

Hero frowned at her. "But then what's the point?"

"The point is, it gives you somewhere to start. And then you meet other people, and you can figure out who you want to be with. And then, if you're lucky, if everything goes okay, you'll get to choose."

"Maybe *you'll* get to choose. I'll never get to choose."

Beatrice shook her head in frustration. "You know, Hero, you think it's so great for me, so easy. But it's not. I mean, it's not hard the way it is for you. But it's still hard."

Hero raised her eyebrows. "Being popular is hard?"

"Yes, it's hard. Everybody's watching you all the time, and you don't feel like yourself anymore."

"What do you mean?"

"Okay. In English last week, the teacher quoted Shakespeare, that line from *Hamlet:* "To sleep, perchance to dream." How many times have we heard Dad say that? And he asked if anyone knew where it was from, and I couldn't raise my hand."

"Why not?"

"Because I'm not like that at school. I'm not the

smart one who knows Shakespeare. Or if I am, I can't be friends with Kelly."

Hero thought about that. "Okay, so it's hard for you, too," she consented. "But, come on, Triss. You wouldn't want to be me."

"Maybe not," Beatrice said impatiently. "But I'm just saying, you wouldn't want to be me either. You would hate it. You would have to change too much about yourself."

That was true, Hero suddenly realized. She would hate being popular. She thought of the poem Mrs. Roth had recited to her. Something about how dreary it was to be somebody. It would be too public, too much attention.

"I guess the best thing is just to be in the middle," Hero said. "Not popular, but not, you know, an outcast."

"Yeah," Beatrice said. "But you still need a way in. Everybody needs that."

Hero sat up, pulling off her socks and starting to get ready for bed. "Well, if you have any ideas, let me know."

"I do," Beatrice said. "I think Danny's your way in."

Remembering all that had happened during the week, Hero couldn't help laughing. "Uh, no. I don't think so. He's sort of the opposite."

Beatrice looked at her questioningly. "Why? In the

eighth grade, he's it. It's weird, but the order of who's popular is totally obvious. And he's different from the rest of them. He doesn't care what they think." She paused. "He's not at your school, so that's a problem. But the kids around here know him, and he likes you. It's going to help you."

"Believe me, Triss," Hero said. "It's not going to help." She couldn't decide how much to tell Beatrice. "They're making fun of me for it. They can't believe he'd hang out with me."

Beatrice's brow furrowed. "Did you tell them you're friends with him?"

Hero couldn't remember what she'd said. All she could remember was trying to end the conversation as quickly as possible. "No, but—"

"Well, geez, Hero, don't deny it. Let them know you're friends with him. Let them wonder what's going on. If you act embarrassed, you're just asking for it."

Hero pulled her nightshirt over her head and shook her hair loose. "Maybe you're right," she conceded. "But it's a little late now."

The thought of school on Monday made her stomach clench with worry. She stretched out on the bed and opened the book her father had given her, trying to concentrate on Edward de Vere. She skimmed the pages quickly, reading about his early childhood, the years at court, the affection of the queen. He was a poet. A scoundrel. An adventurer. Could he have been Shakespeare? Was there any way to know for sure?

CHAPTER 20

On Monday, Hero lingered in the hallway outside her classroom. She had decided to wait until the last possible minute to go in. That way, maybe she could avoid the morning chatter and whatever else lay in store for her. As the other kids crowded past her, she tried to look engrossed in the bulletin board, haphazardly covered—just before Parents' Night—with essays on the Salem witch trials.

Mrs. Vanderley appeared in the classroom doorway. "Oh, Hero. Good. I was afraid you were absent. You're wanted down at the principal's office."

"I am?" Hero looked at her in alarm.

"Yes, they just buzzed. Go right now so you'll be back in time for Math."

Hero started down the hallway, her heart pounding. What now? She'd never been to the principal's office, not once in her entire life. She didn't even know what one looked like. She hurried to the main office, where she and Aaron had stopped on the first day of school. The secretary smiled at her.

"How can I help you?" she asked pleasantly.

Hero swallowed. "Um, I . . . I think I'm supposed to see the principal."

"Oh." The secretary checked a calendar on her desk. "Your name?"

"Hero Netherfield."

"Oh, yes, go on in. Mrs. Rivnor's expecting you."

Hero looked around in bewilderment, at the chairs and desks and the many nondescript brown doors leading to offices on all sides. "I don't know where to go."

The secretary smiled again. "You don't? Well, I suppose that's a good thing. Some of the students know their way blindfolded." She gestured to the door behind her.

Hero felt so nervous she thought she might faint. She took a deep breath and cautiously opened the door.

Mrs. Rivnor was sitting behind her desk, writing briskly on a yellow notepad. She was a large woman, with graying hair and bright red glasses that slipped to the end of her nose. Hero could remember seeing her in the hallway during the first week of school and once at an assembly, but she had no other impression of her. She waited, but Mrs. Rivnor continued writing. Finally, she looked up.

"Yes?"

Hero clutched her backpack and tried to keep her voice steady. "Mrs. Vanderley said you wanted to see me."

Mrs. Rivnor gestured at the chair in front of her desk. "Oh, yes. You're Hero Netherfield? Sit down, please. You and I need to talk about a few things."

Hero shuffled warily to the chair and sat on the very edge of it. She held her backpack on her lap, pillowed against her chest. What could they possibly need to talk about?

Mrs. Rivnor leaned back in her chair and rested her pen on the pad in front of her. She considered Hero for a minute, then said crisply, "When I arrived at school this morning, one of our custodians informed me that a stall in the boys' bathroom was vandalized over the weekend. The wall was spray-painted black."

Hero's heart pounded so loudly that she thought the sound would fill the entire room. She looked at the floor. Danny had done it.

"I understand from various sources that this particular stall had been vandalized with graffiti last week and that your name appeared in the, mmm, vulgar commentary. I assume you were aware of that." She was watching Hero closely.

Hero nodded, not knowing what to say.

Mrs. Rivnor picked up her pen, rolling it lightly in her palm. "Did you inform your teacher about the graffiti? Did you report it to anyone here in the office?"

Hero looked up. "No . . ."

"And so you took matters into your own hands."

"No—"

"Listen to me carefully, Hero." Mrs. Rivnor leaned forward, and Hero realized, nervously, that she was very angry. "I understand that in many schools, what those boys wrote about you in the bathroom would have gone unnoticed by the administration, a 'boys will be boys' attitude. But *not* in my school. I will not tolerate that kind of uncivil, abusive, harassing behavior among my students." She rapped her pen sharply on the desk. Hero jumped in her chair.

"I am sorry that you did not have enough confidence in me, as your principal, to approach me about this situation."

Hero nodded meekly. "I didn't know—"

"I realize that you were probably embarrassed and upset by this. But let me remind you that now, instead of ballpoint graffiti, my custodial staff has some kind of permanent black paint to contend with." Mrs. Rivnor grimaced in annoyance. "I am not going to ask you if you were involved in this vandalism, Hero. And I am not going to ask you if you know who was involved. I am going to tell you what I intend to do."

Hero sat back in the chair, clutching her backpack for protection.

"I have spoken to Mrs. Vanderley. There will be no more teasing or harassment of any kind in the classroom. That is not acceptable behavior under any circumstances, and children who participate in that kind of"—Mrs. Rivnor drew herself up indignantly—"persecution will be severely punished. I have instructed all of the teachers to speak to their classes about tolerance and respect for others, and to observe the students closely for violations of school policy."

Mrs. Rivnor paused, studying Hero. "I realize that you are new to our school, Hero. Perhaps that explains the breach in protocol in this matter. But in the future, if something of this nature arises, I hope you will feel that you can turn to this school's administration for support."

Hero nodded. "I'm—"

"Every child at Ogden Elementary is entitled to learn in a safe and respectful environment."

"I—"

"Your teacher, Mrs. Vanderley, and I are here to make sure that your experience at Ogden is a good one, Hero. We will listen to your concerns."

"That's—"

"Do you understand?" Mrs. Rivnor lifted her pen again, writing something on the yellow pad. "Is there anything you'd like to say to me?"

Hero took a deep breath, startled by the silence in the room. "No," she said quietly. "I'm sorry about the bathroom."

"All right then. Would you like me to schedule a conference with your parents about this harassment issue?"

Hero shuddered. "No, please—"

Mrs. Rivnor nodded briskly. "Then I believe we're finished. Let's get you back to class before you miss any more instructional time." She stood up and strode to the door, holding it open for Hero.

"Thanks," said Hero, feeling dazed.

She wandered out of the office, her backpack dangling from one hand. She thought about Danny, climbing through the bathroom window last night with his can of spray paint. Mrs. Rivnor was right. It was vandalism. And Mrs. Roth was right. It was the wrong thing to do. And Triss was right. Danny must not care what anyone thought. But suddenly, none of it mattered. Danny Cordova had done this for *her*.

CHAPTER 21

When Hero stepped off the bus that afternoon, she saw Danny leaning against the street sign, talking to his friends. She walked quickly over to him, ignoring the look that Aaron's brother gave her.

"Hey, Danny," she said quietly. "Thanks."

He smiled at her. "Sure. No problem."

As Hero turned away, she heard him say something to the other boys. A minute later, he was walking beside her.

"So it worked?" he asked.

Hero thought he looked a little smug. "Well, I had to go to the principal's office this morning," she said. "But it was okay. I mean, she was almost more upset about what they wrote than I was." She laughed, remembering. Then she stopped. "What did they write?"

Danny glanced at her. "Oh, you know. The usual." He grinned. "Maybe I should have left it there. It might have made you more popular."

Hero gave him a shove, but he only laughed at her, unfazed, his blond hair flopping over his forehead. "You going to Miriam's?"

Hero nodded. "Are you coming?"

"Sure, in a while." He turned back to his friends.

When Hero reached Mrs. Roth's, she found her stooping over a flower bed, pulling weeds. A handful of roots and grasses lay in a sodden pile at her feet.

"Hey," Hero called. "I can do that."

"Oh, that's all right, Hero." Mrs. Roth smiled at her, flexing her hands and rubbing the knuckles. "You and I have more important things to do. Come see what I found."

She led the way to the porch, where *Tudor England* was splayed open, pages ruffling in the breeze. "Look at this."

Hero could hear the excitement in her voice. She sat on the step and lifted the book into her lap, glancing at a page crowded with portraits of Queen Elizabeth in all her usual regalia. "I know," she said. "I've found lots of pictures of her, too. She's always wearing those dresses that look like they'd weigh a ton."

Mrs. Roth pointed, her smile widening. "Look at her necklace in this one."

Hero bent closer to the page. It was hard to see the necklace. "There's no pendant," she said, squinting.

"No," Mrs. Roth said. "But look at the necklace itself, the pattern of pearls and rubies."

"Is it our necklace?" Hero gasped. She tilted the page in the sunlight. "Do you think it is?" She jiggled the heavy book on her knees. "But how did Queen Elizabeth . . ."

"From her mother, of course. From Anne Boleyn."

Hero nodded slowly, beginning to piece it together. "But where's the pendant?"

"Well, I've been thinking about that." Mrs. Roth gripped the post and lowered herself to the step. "Anne Boleyn was tried for adultery and executed for treason. Elizabeth's own position was not at all secure. There were lots of people plotting against her. She knew how easily she might suffer the same fate as her poor mother. So I think she would have been careful not to wear something the public would recognize as Anne Boleyn's. The pendant is very distinctive, and of course her mother's crest was on the back of it."

"That makes sense," Hero agreed.

Mrs. Roth touched her arm. "There's more." She turned the pages to a section of the book marked with a torn piece of paper. "Look at this. It's a poem Elizabeth wrote when she was twenty, while she was under arrest at Woodstock, held for suspected treason."

Hero read aloud:

"Much suspected by me,
Nothing proved can be,
Quoth Elizabeth prisoner."

Hero looked at Mrs. Roth, puzzled. "I didn't know she wrote poetry, but I don't see . . ."

Mrs. Roth tapped the page. Hero glanced down again and felt a chill go through her. The caption under the poem read: *"Written with a diamond on her window at Woodstock."*

"I don't understand," Hero said.

Mrs. Roth beamed. "She used a diamond to write on the window glass. She scratched out the words. She was a prisoner; perhaps she didn't have pen and paper, or perhaps she wanted to leave a permanent record."

"But is it *the* diamond?" Hero asked. "The Murphy diamond?"

"I doubt we'll ever know." Mrs. Roth shifted the

book from Hero's lap into her own. "But it could be. She was a prisoner, accused of a crime. Why would she have jewels with her? Unless it was one particular jewel, the pendant left to her by her dead mother—"

Hero interrupted breathlessly, "And that's what I have to tell you. I talked to my dad about Edward de Vere, and he said the connection wasn't with Anne Boleyn, it was with Elizabeth. I guess people think they might have been in love or something." She tried to remember all the details. "I've been reading about him. His father died when he was little, so he was raised by one of her royal advisors. He was Elizabeth's favorite at the court, and she even gave him money, a thousand pounds a year, when he grew up."

"Really?" Mrs. Roth's eyes widened. "He might have been her lover? But that seems unlikely, doesn't it? If he was born in 1550, he was seventeen years younger than Elizabeth."

Hero laughed. "Yeah, she'd be old enough to be his mother."

Mrs. Roth looked at her strangely. "What did you say?"

"She'd be old enough to be his mother. Back then, they had kids kind of young, right?"

Mrs. Roth nodded slowly, turning the pages of the

book. "His mother." She paused, looking at Hero. "What if she were his mother?"

"But she didn't have any children," Hero said. She hesitated. "Unless it was a secret. Unless nobody knew." She stared at the book.

"When was Edward de Vere born again?" Mrs. Roth asked.

"In 1550. Or around there. My dad says the dates aren't very accurate."

"So what happened to Elizabeth in 1550? Let's see, there was something when she was a teenager, some scandal," Mrs. Roth flipped the pages. "Ah yes, here it is, in 1548 or 1549. She was living in the house of Catherine Parr—you remember, the last wife of Henry VIII—who had remarried. And there was something involving Catherine Parr's husband or another man. Some impropriety. It sounds as though nobody knew exactly what happened, but Elizabeth was forced to leave the house afterward."

"They kicked her out?" Hero turned to Mrs. Roth suddenly, grabbing her sleeve. "Do you think . . . do you think she got pregnant? Could that be it?" She bounced to her feet. "Because if she were Edward de Vere's mother . . . if she were his mother, then Anne Boleyn would be his grandmother!"

"And it would make sense, perfect sense, for Edward de Vere to inherit his grandmother's necklace," Mrs. Roth finished for her. They looked at each other in astonishment.

Hero shook her head slowly. She felt a strange thrill running through her. "Not only that," she said. "It's more than that. My dad kept saying there was no proof of the relationship between Elizabeth and Edward de Vere, why they were so close. But what if the necklace is the proof?"

"You mean the proof that Edward de Vere was Elizabeth's son?" Mrs. Roth asked.

"And the reason that everything had to be kept secret." Hero began to pace in front of the porch. "Shakespeare's plays. If Edward de Vere wrote all those plays, but he was the queen's son, he couldn't put his name on anything."

"Yes," said Mrs. Roth. She looked at Hero, her eyes wide. "Your father said the royals believed playwriting was beneath them. If Edward de Vere was the queen's son, her *illegitimate* son no less, it would have been even more important to hide his authorship. She wouldn't have wanted him to attract attention. It might have exposed their relationship."

"And don't forget the money," Hero added, hopping

from one foot to the other. "The thousand pounds. Maybe she paid him that to keep him from telling anyone about his writing."

"Yes," Mrs. Roth said. "As compensation for staying anonymous, because she wasn't going to have her own son earn his living by writing plays for commoners." She shook her head in wonder. "Oh, Hero! I'm remembering the plays, all the details of royal life, the intrigues of the court."

Hero nodded excitedly. "My dad said that the real Shakespeare was just an ordinary businessman who shouldn't have known about all that."

"And all the plays about slander or betrayal," Mrs. Roth continued. "Think of your play, *Much Ado About Nothing*. Hero must fake her death because of a false accusation. If that were Shakespeare's secret—that he was really Elizabeth's son and Anne Boleyn's grandson—all of his writing about slander would be even more powerful. The reason his grandmother died. The reason his mother was imprisoned."

"And it all fits," Hero said, barely able to contain herself. "I mean, there isn't much known about Edward de Vere's parents, and he grew up as Elizabeth's favorite . . . Oh, Mrs. Roth! What if the necklace is the key to everything?"

Mrs. Roth squeezed her hand. "Think of it! What if we've discovered the secret identity of William Shakespeare?"

Hero looked up and saw Danny about to turn in the gate. "Here comes Danny," she whispered quickly. "I didn't tell him about the necklace. I thought you wouldn't want me to because of his dad. He knows we're looking for the diamond, but that's all."

CHAPTER 22

"Hey," Danny called to them, glancing at the yard. "You weren't weeding, were you, Miriam? Let me do that."

"Oh, would you?" Mrs. Roth smiled at him gratefully. "That would be lovely. I'll get us some refreshments."

Mrs. Roth went inside, and Hero joined Danny in the garden. She tried not to think about the necklace, but her heart was racing. She was afraid she'd say something she shouldn't. They crouched side by side, yanking tufts of grass from the dark, loose earth beneath the rosebushes.

"So your dad doesn't know you took the spray paint?" Hero asked. "You won't get in trouble for that, will you?"

Danny shook his head. "I didn't use that much.

And my dad's got a lot of other stuff to worry about." He smiled a little. "That's the good thing about having only one parent around. He's not watching my every move, you know? He doesn't have time."

"Do you ever see your mom?" Hero asked. "Do you visit her?"

Danny shook his head. "I haven't seen her since she left."

"Don't you miss her?"

Danny shrugged. "I was five when she left. I don't remember her that well." He hesitated. "I mean, I do. I remember how she looked. But sometimes I don't know if I really remember, or if I just know how she looked from the pictures. We have pictures of her all over the place. My dad hung them up. So I wouldn't forget, I guess." He sat back on his heels. "I remember how she smelled, and I remember games we played. But I don't remember how I felt about her. Isn't that weird?"

Hero didn't know what to say. It was strange not to know how you felt about your mom. But it wasn't strange to forget how you felt about someone who disappeared years ago. "Well," she said after a minute. "You were five, right? You were really little."

"Yeah."

"So why did she leave?" Hero asked.

"She just left." Danny pulled up a fistful of crabgrass, banging it against the flagstone. The ball of dirt around the roots crumbled, and he brushed it back into the flower bed.

Hero waited.

"She got tired . . . you know, tired of being a mom."

Hero had never heard of such a thing. She stared at him. "Really?"

"That's what my dad says." Danny hesitated. "Well, he doesn't say that exactly. He says she got tired of her life. She couldn't stand her life. But, I mean, she was at home with me all the time, so . . ." He left the question hanging in the air.

Hero looked at him, wanting to help. She thought of her own brisk, good-natured mother, who was so annoying at times but at least always there. "Maybe it was something with your dad," she said. "There are lots of reasons she could have left." She yanked a leggy weed from the dense shock of tiger lilies. "And now she's in California?"

"Yeah, L.A. She wants to be an actress." Danny collected the weeds at his feet and tossed them onto Hero's pile. "You know, acting, you can't do that around here. You pretty much have to be in L.A."

"That makes sense." Hero nodded, watching him. "Well, how's she doing? Has she made any movies?"

"Not yet, but she's done some commercials. She's trying to break into the film stuff. It's hard. She doesn't have any money. But I think she'll make it. My mom's really beautiful."

"She is?"

He nodded firmly. "Definitely."

Hero stood up, stretching. "It must be hard for you," she said hesitantly.

Danny wiped his face on his T-shirt, leaving a damp brown streak across it. "Sometimes. But she wasn't happy here. My dad says she was never happy."

The screen door creaked open, and Mrs. Roth stepped out, balancing a tray.

"Oh, look at you two!" she said approvingly. "You've finished two beds. It would have taken me all afternoon to get that far. Come have something to drink."

They all settled on the porch steps, and Hero held the cold glass against her face. The tea tasted cool and sweet, with a lemony sharpness. The china plate was heaped with cookies this time, chocolate chip. Danny took four. Hero rested one on her knee. They all looked across the garden to the Netherfields' house.

"So where do you think the diamond is?" Danny asked. "In the house? In the yard? It's a big diamond, right? It shouldn't be so hard to find."

Mrs. Roth sighed. "Maybe we're wrong," she said. "Maybe it's not there at all."

"But the note—" Hero protested, then bit her lip.

Danny looked at Mrs. Roth with interest. "What note?"

Mrs. Roth glanced at Hero. "Well, I suppose the cat's out of the bag on that one. But, Daniel, I'd prefer not to answer police questions about this."

"Oh, come on, Miriam. I told you, I won't say anything. I promise. And my dad won't ask me. It's not like he's still working on it."

Mrs. Roth went into the house and returned a few minutes later. She held out the note card to Danny, angling it carefully so that he could only read the back. "It's from Arthur," she explained. "We think it has something to do with where the diamond is hidden."

Danny peered at the card, frowning. "I don't get it."

Mrs. Roth shook her head in mock disapproval. "Now, Daniel, aren't you in the eighth grade? I thought Hero told me that English literature is part of the curriculum by then. It's by Dylan Thomas, a very famous poem he wrote to his dying father." She read it aloud:

"Do not go gentle into that good night.
Rage, rage against the dying of the light."

"So that's our clue," Hero explained to Danny. "The only one we have."

"Okay." Danny reached for another cookie and chewed it thoughtfully. "What does it mean?"

They sat in silence. Hero watched Mrs. Roth cover the card gently with her pale hands.

"'Rage against the dying of the light,'" Danny repeated.

Hero nodded. "So we thought, something that fights death."

"Or something that fights the dark," Danny said. "Like a light."

Hero looked at him. She looked at Mrs. Roth. She felt a strange, thrilling flip in her stomach.

"A light," she repeated, staring at the side of her house. "There are lots of lights. Lots of old, glass lights on the ceilings. Could it be hidden inside one of those?"

Mrs. Roth opened her palms, staring at the writing, stark on the creamy paper. She turned to Hero. "Could that be it?" she asked softly. "Are they like the ones at my house? When you change a lightbulb, do you unscrew a knob to remove the glass bowl?"

"I don't know. I've never done it."

"The fixtures are so ornate, made of cut glass. It does seem possible." She touched Danny's shoulder. "And it would be just like Arthur, too, to be literal. Not 'the dying of the light' as metaphor, as death, but literally the light being turned out."

Hero scrambled to her feet. "We have to start looking! Let's go."

"What about your parents?" Danny asked. "We should wait till no one's around."

Mrs. Roth nodded. "You can't be ransacking the house beneath their very noses," she said gently. "Certainly not without an explanation."

Hero slumped in disappointment, but then she brightened. "They have a party Friday night. And Triss has a sleepover. But that's so far away."

Mrs. Roth smiled, her eyes soft. "Oh, Hero. Think of the diamond. What if we've found it?" She took Hero's hand and curled it into a fist. "What if the next time I see you, you're holding it here in your hand?"

CHAPTER 23

For the entire week, while she waited for Friday, Hero thought of nothing but the diamond. At school, the teasing had miraculously subsided. She wasn't exactly sure why. Maybe it was the brief scolding by Mrs. Vanderley about the need to respect fellow students. Or the impending school assembly on harassment. But more likely, it was Danny's paint job in the bathroom, which had caused its own stir. Hero could tell that the other kids viewed her warily now. It wasn't "the way in" that Beatrice had promised, but it was something—a way out of the other situation.

And it let Hero focus all her attention on her real interest. She spent her school days doodling sharp-sided, glittering diamonds in the margins of her notebooks, sometimes connecting them in a long jewel-laden necklace. She kept imagining the feel of it, the cold, heavy weight in her hand.

It was the same at home. Hero found herself wandering from room to room, staring at the light fixtures so intently that even her mother noticed.

"Is there a spider up there?"

"Uh, no," Hero answered quickly. "I was just thinking that we have really pretty lights in this house."

"And since when are you so interested in interior decor? Does your newfound curiosity about history extend to architectural detail, too?"

"Sort of."

Her mother shook her head, smiling. "Well, do our electricity bill a favor and try to remember to turn *off* the light when you're finished appreciating its finer features."

"Oh, sure, Mom. Sorry."

⋄ ⋄ ⋄

On Friday evening, Hero lay on the bed in her parents' room, watching them get ready for the party. The air was heavy with hair spray and cologne, and Hero pulled her shirt over her nose so she could breathe.

Her mother leaned across the dresser toward the

mirror, holding up two different earrings. "Which one?" she asked Hero.

"The gold looks better."

"Really? Maybe you're right."

Hero rolled on her back and studied the light in the middle of her parents' ceiling. Like the others in the house, it was etched glass, with grooves and ridges outlining little flowers. At the base was a brass knob. If a diamond were hidden there, wouldn't it show? Wouldn't there be a shadow, some shape against the glass? Her eyes began to hurt from staring at it so long. She turned back to her mother, squinting against the dark blotches that clouded her vision. She thought about her conversation with Danny.

"Do you ever get tired of being a mom?" she asked.

Her mother laughed. "What do you mean?"

"Do you get tired of it? Do you ever just want to quit?"

Her mother sat next to her and slipped her feet into her stockings, unfurling them along her legs. "Well, I get tired of making lunches. I would be perfectly happy not to make another sandwich for the rest of my life."

"So you do get tired of being a mom?" Hero persisted.

Her mother shook her head. "No, I don't think

that's possible. I think you get tired of something you do, not something you are."

Hero thought for a minute. "Triss and I could make our own lunches," she offered.

"Yes, you could, couldn't you? But my mother always did it for me, so I suppose I can do it for you. It's not a big deal." Her mother stood up, smoothing her dress. "What do you think?"

"You look good," Hero said.

"Thank you. Too much perfume?"

"Well, sure. Always."

Her father leaned out of the bathroom, adjusting his tie. "You think I'm wearing too much perfume?" he asked.

Hero laughed. "No, you should wear more."

"I prefer a subtle effect, unlike your mother."

Her mother rolled her eyes. "Did Beatrice leave already?" she asked Hero.

"Yeah, a while ago. She yelled up to you. Didn't you hear her?"

Her mother shook her head in disgust. "You girls never let me know what you're up to."

Hero hesitated. She knew she should tell them about Danny coming over. But they wouldn't understand, and she couldn't explain the real reason. She would tell them later, she decided.

"Why are you getting all dressed up?" she asked, watching her mother slide on her pumps and check herself in the mirror. "What's the party?"

"It's the opening of that new exhibit at the Maxwell," said her mother. "Remember, I designed the invitations?"

Hero vaguely recalled the crimson print. "Oh, yeah," she said. "But what's the exhibit?"

Her father sat on the edge of the bed, holding one shoe. "*Hamlet* Revisited: Displays of the Bad Quarto, the Good Quarto, and the Folios."

Hero sighed. It might as well have been another language. "What's a bad quarto?" she couldn't help asking.

"It's a very early printed version of the play. The text is a bit different from the later Folio versions, and the meaning of *Hamlet* changes depending on which one you read."

"Why would anybody read the bad version?" Hero wanted to know.

Her father laughed. "It's not really 'bad.' It's just a different, early version, and people think there are errors in it."

Hero rolled on her stomach, resting her chin in her hands. "And that's the whole exhibit? Just a bunch of copies of the play?"

"Oh, no. There's scholarly interpretation, of course, and various period artifacts—costumes, portraiture, that sort of thing."

"But I thought it was a library. How did the Maxwell get all that other stuff?"

Her father stood up. "The same way we get most of our documents. The same way we got the Bad Quarto. We bought it. That's what the endowment is for."

"Does it cost a lot of money?"

"Yes, of course. Some of the pieces are worth millions."

Hero looked at the bedside clock. It was almost seven. She twisted her hair restlessly. "When does the party start?"

Her mother glanced at her. "Don't worry, we'll be out of your way in no time."

Her father laughed. "'How poor are they that have not patience!'"

Hero made a face at him and kept fiddling with her hair. She would call Danny as soon as they left.

CHAPTER 24

When Danny appeared at the back door, Hero grabbed his sleeve and dragged him through the kitchen. "Come on, come on! It took you forever to get here."

"I didn't even have dinner yet," Danny protested. He stopped at the cupboard next to the refrigerator. "Is there anything to eat in here?"

"Like what?"

"I don't know. Cookies?"

"Can't you wait till we're finished?"

"No. I'm really hungry."

"Oh, geez." Hero swung open the cupboard. "No cookies. What do you want? Cinnamon toast?"

They both laughed.

"Yeah, what's the deal with Miriam and cinnamon toast?" Danny asked. "It's like she's making money on it. I almost fell over when she gave us cookies last time."

Hero shrugged, feeling suddenly protective of Mrs. Roth. "She just likes it, I guess. I do, too. It reminds me of when I was little."

She reached into the cupboard, sorting through boxes of tea and jars of spices until she found a bag of chocolate chips. "How about these?"

Danny ripped the foil package and dumped a small pile on the counter between them. "So how's it been at school?" he asked, his mouth full.

Hero thought for a minute. "Well, nobody really talks to me. But they don't bug me now either, so I guess it's getting better."

Danny shook his head. "You know, you and Triss are really different from each other."

Hero stiffened with irritation. She hadn't expected this from him. "I know. We don't look anything alike." She rolled up the bag of chocolate chips and shoved it back into the cupboard.

Danny looked annoyed. "That's not what I mean. What I mean is, Triss sort of, well, she *lets* people like her. She lets people make friends with her. You walk around looking like you expect everybody to pick on you. And then they kind of do."

"Thanks, Danny. That makes me feel a lot better."

"No, I'm just saying—"

"I get it, okay? Stop acting like a guidance counselor." Hero pushed him ahead of her into the dining room. She suddenly wanted him to go home. But she knew she needed help with the lights.

Danny shot her a glance. "Listen, Netherfield . . . just forget it," he said.

"I will," Hero answered, frowning. "Let's start looking. My mom and dad said they'd be back by midnight."

The dining room was dark. Hero slid the light switch, and the chandelier glowed brightly.

Danny scrutinized it. "Can't be in there," he decided. "There's no place to put it."

"No," Hero agreed. "But the other ones are different."

She led him into the tiny study, which was awash in yellow light. In the middle of the ceiling was a round glass fixture etched with a floral pattern. Danny reached up to unscrew it, then jumped back with a yelp. "Ow! It's hot! Turn off the light."

Hero flipped the switch, and they stood uncertainly in the dark.

"Now I can't see anything," Danny complained.

"I'll put the hall light on."

After a few minutes, Danny began to unscrew the

knob again, touching it gingerly. Slowly he lowered the glass bowl and looked inside.

"Oh my God," he said in a hushed voice.

"You found it?" Hero gasped.

"No, but there's a dead bug in here." He laughed at her, overturning the bowl and tapping the bug onto the carpet.

"Stop fooling around," Hero snapped.

"Hey, you're a little uptight."

"Well, geez, Danny. It's the Murphy diamond! This isn't a joke."

"I know. But the thing I can't figure out is, do you really think Murphy'd hide it inside a light? I mean, people change their lightbulbs. Anybody could have found it by now."

Hero sighed. "There was nobody living here most of last year. Don't you think it's the kind of place the police wouldn't look?"

"Yeah, sure. Because the police would say, 'People change their lightbulbs all the time, that'd be a dumb hiding place.'"

Hero scowled at him, turning away. "Finding place," she said absently.

Danny looked at her, fitting the light fixture back into place. "Why do you call it that?"

"I don't. Mrs. Roth said her daughter used to call it that, when they played hide-and-seek."

"Yeah, I remember," Danny said. "I always called it that too. But I thought my mom and I were the only ones."

Hero shrugged. "Maybe it's a Maryland thing."

She stood in the doorway, surveying the rooms that opened into the front hall. "The hall light's different. It kind of looks like a lantern. It can't be inside that. And there's not a ceiling light in the living room. So that leaves the bathroom down here, and then the upstairs lights."

They crowded into the bathroom. Hero boosted herself onto the sink, the porcelain cold on her palms. Danny flipped down the toilet lid with a clunk and climbed on top of it. He carefully unscrewed the fixture, lowering it with one hand. Hero waited.

"Nope," he said, screwing it back in place.

Discouraged, they headed upstairs. They went from room to room, standing unsteadily in the middle of the beds to reach the light fixtures. Each time, one of them would unscrew the brass knob and lower the bowl, and they would both peer hopefully inside, to find nothing but dust and the occasional dead insect, its papery wings stuck to the glass.

Beatrice's room was last. Hero clambered onto the mattress, her feet sinking into the soft cotton of the bedspread. As she turned the knob, Danny hopped up next to her. He began to bounce lightly, shaking the whole bed.

"Cut it out," Hero complained, trying not to laugh.

"Oh, come on, Netherfield," he said, bouncing harder. Hero giggled, trying to keep her balance. Then, suddenly, she lost her grip on the brass knob. It dropped to the bed and the glass bowl slid heavily after it. Hero and Danny both grabbed at it frantically, but they only succeeded in knocking it with a crash to the floor.

"Uh oh," said Danny.

Hero covered her face with her hands. "Did it break?" she asked, afraid to look.

"Pretty much."

Hero leaned over the edge of the bed. The fixture lay in pieces next to Beatrice's nightstand, its beautiful leafy vines broken into jagged chunks.

"Oh no."

"Sorry." Danny crouched down and gathered the pieces in his hand. "Maybe we can glue it."

Hero moaned. "This is a disaster. What am I going to tell Triss? And what about my parents?"

"Tell them you were trying to change the lightbulb."

"Like they will ever in a million years believe that!"

"Well, what else are you going to say? You can't tell them about the diamond. Look, let's try to glue it. Maybe nobody'll even notice."

"Danny, it's broken in five pieces! I think they'll notice."

"Listen, if you have a better idea, let me know. But it's almost eleven, and you said your parents would be back before midnight."

"It's eleven o'clock? You have to get out of here!" Hero snatched the glass fragments and slid them gingerly under Beatrice's bed. "Just go. I'll figure something out."

She rushed Danny down the stairs ahead of her, hurrying through the kitchen.

Danny stopped at the back door.

"So what do you think? It's not in the house, I guess."

Hero glanced around her, at the shadow-filled hall, the glowing doorway of the dining room, the bright yellow glare from the bathroom.

"I don't know," she said. "Maybe you're right. Mr. Murphy wouldn't put the diamond someplace where it could be found by just anybody."

"No," Danny agreed. He swung open the door, and the cool night air flooded the kitchen, fresh and sharp and smelling faintly of flowers. Across the driveway, Hero could barely make out the dark lines of Mrs. Roth's fence. She shivered.

"All right, go on," she said quickly. "Before my parents get back. I have to turn off the lights now and make sure they don't look in the bedroom."

But Danny didn't answer. He was standing on the porch, staring at something.

"You have one of those lights out here, too," he said. Hero saw that he was looking at the porch light, its chiseled glass bowl densely covered with roses.

"Yeah, but we don't know where the switch is," Hero said. "This switch in the kitchen is just for the lights on the side." She flipped it, and the floodlights on either side of the porch sent bold arcs of light across the driveway.

"You don't know where the switch is?" Danny repeated.

"No," Hero said slowly. "So we never turn it on." She stared at the light. "Remember what it said on the card? *Do not go gentle into that good night.*"

They looked at each other. Hero swallowed hard. "You should go," she said faintly, but it didn't sound convincing even to her.

"Do it," Danny said.

"I can't reach it."

"I'll help you." Before she could protest, Danny boosted her onto the porch railing. He held her legs as she stood. Hero stretched toward the light, reaching for the knob at its base. Her hands were shaking. She felt the warmth of Danny's shoulder pressing against her legs as she unscrewed it. Carefully, breathlessly, she lowered the glass bowl. She thought she heard something rattle.

"Is it there?" Danny's voice was soft and urgent.

"I don't know, I can't see. Help me down."

Danny steadied her as she crouched down on the railing, the glass cupped in her hands. Together they leaned over the bowl. There, in the bottom, caught in the pale band of light from the kitchen doorway, was something hard and clear and flashing, despite the dust that had settled thickly around it.

"Oh—" said Hero.

"Wow," said Danny.

They knew in an instant that they were looking at the Murphy diamond.

CHAPTER 25

Hero thought she might faint. She grabbed Danny's arm to steady herself.

"Is that it? Is that really it?" she whispered.

"Pick it up," Danny said softly.

Hero jumped down from the porch rail, clutching the glass, and lifted the diamond from the bowl. It was a little bigger than a quarter, but full of angles. It felt heavy and smooth in her hand, almost silky. She rubbed it gently on her shirt, then held it in the light of the doorway. It sparkled, each edge glinting tiny rays of golden light.

"It's beautiful," Hero breathed.

Danny took it from her. His fingers closed tightly around it, his hand dropping to his side.

"What are you doing?" Hero asked.

"I should go," he said. "Your parents will be home soon."

"But the diamond—" Hero protested.

"It's better if I take it with me." His voice was low, insistent. "What if your parents find it? Or Triss? They'll make us give it back. They don't know about everything else."

"But your father. Don't you think—"

"I'll take care of it. Leave it to me." There was something in Danny's eyes that Hero had not seen before, a softness, a kind of pleading.

She hesitated. "Okay," she said reluctantly. "But, Danny . . . be careful."

"I will," he promised. He slid the diamond into his jeans pocket, then took the glass from Hero.

"Screw the cover back on, quick," he ordered, helping her back onto the railing. As she finished twisting the knob, Hero saw headlights at the end of the driveway.

"Go, Danny. Hurry!" she cried, hopping down. He ran down the porch steps and sprinted along the driveway into the shadowy darkness of the front yard. Hero went quickly into the house, slamming the kitchen door behind her. She rushed from room to room, frantically turning off lights. In Beatrice's room, she stopped in despair, staring at the naked bulb that blazed with neon intensity in the middle of the ceiling. How was she ever going to explain this?

Downstairs, she heard the door open and the muffled sounds of her parents entering, keys scattering on the table, her mother's purse dropping with a thud.

"Hero? Where are you?" Her father's voice echoed up the stairs. "It's dark in here."

She heard her mother in the hall. "I didn't expect you to take my warning about the electricity bill so seriously."

Hero took a deep breath. "I'm upstairs," she called.

She flipped off Beatrice's light and went downstairs. Her father sat at the kitchen table, loosening his tie, while her mother filled the teakettle.

"How was the party?" Hero asked.

"Nice." "Long." Her parents answered simultaneously, then laughed.

"We wanted to leave an hour ago," her mother said. "Did everything go okay here?"

Hero tried to sound casual. "Fine. Danny came over for a while."

"What?" Her mother and father both turned to her.

"Not for very long," she said quickly.

Her parents exchanged glances. "Hero." Her

mother's voice was sharp. "Did his parents know he was at our house, without any adults?"

"Oh, Mom," Hero said. "We were just hanging out."

Her father looked at her. "Ah yes, the ubiquitous 'hanging out.' What does that mean, exactly?"

"You know, hanging around."

"Well, that certainly clarifies the matter."

Her mother's lips narrowed to a thin line. She poured the steaming water into two mugs. She didn't say anything.

Hero waited in the doorway, trying to calm her jittery nerves, thinking about the diamond, and Danny, and everything else that had happened. "Sorry," she said, meaning it.

Her mother studied her for a minute. "Look, Hero," she said finally. "We trust you. I hope you won't do anything to make us change our minds about that."

"I won't," Hero promised. She felt vaguely guilty, but at the same time, flattered.

"Tea?" her mother asked.

"No, I'm going to bed. I'm kind of tired." Hero kissed them quickly and left the room, before they could ask more questions. At least Beatrice wouldn't be back till tomorrow morning. That gave her time to think up an excuse about the light.

In her own room, she slipped out of her jeans and shirt and pulled on her nightshirt, tugging the elastic band out of her hair. She sat on the edge of her bed in the dark, thinking about the diamond. It seemed like a dream now, almost unbelievable to her that they'd found it. Danny was right, she decided. It would be safer with him. She thought of its sharp angles, its cool heft in her palm. What would Mrs. Roth say?

Hero couldn't wait to give it to her. She couldn't wait to see it settled where it belonged, in Anne Boleyn's sparkling necklace. Mrs. Roth would be so happy! After so much time, after so much sadness, the Murphy diamond had finally been found.

CHAPTER 26

When Hero awoke the next morning, sunlight flooded the bedroom. She couldn't believe that she'd slept late on this of all mornings. She had to tell Mrs. Roth about the diamond! She threw off the blankets impatiently and pulled on her clothing, leaving her pajamas in a cottony pool on the bedroom floor. She had just dragged a brush through her hair when her mother leaned in the doorway.

"Where are you off to in such a hurry?"

"I'm going over to Mrs. Roth's."

"At ten thirty in the morning?"

"Is it that late? I have to go."

"Not without making your bed, I hope."

Hero groaned and quickly pulled the covers over the bed, dodging past her mother before she could think of another chore.

Outside, the air was crisp and beginning to smell like autumn. One of the big shade trees in the front yard had a bright patch of orange creeping through the green. Hero yanked her sweater tightly around her and ran down the driveway. When she reached the street, she heard distant laughter. Down at the corner, she saw Danny and his friends.

What was he doing down there? She ran toward them, shouting his name.

The group of boys shifted slightly, looking at her. Aaron's brother Ben and the other boy smirked, but Danny just stood where he was, sliding his skateboard back and forth with one foot.

"Hey, Cordova," Ben said. "Your little girlfriend wants you."

Hero blushed but ignored him, running up to Danny. She grabbed his arm.

"Come on, we have to go see Mrs. Roth. I thought you'd be there already."

Danny looked away. "You go ahead," he said to Hero. "I'll catch you later."

"But—" Hero protested.

"Later." He said again, moving away. Hero hesitated. She looked over at the two boys, who were still smirking, then at Danny who had suddenly absorbed himself in picking a leaf off the wheel of his skateboard. What was going on? Why was he acting like this? Hero felt a thin, sharp prick of anger.

"Look, don't bother," she said testily. "But," she swallowed hard, "you have something I need."

Ben and the other boy hooted with laughter. "Oooo, you have something she needs, Cordova. Something she *needs*."

Hero turned to Ben angrily. "Shut up! Just shut up! This is none of your business."

Ben leaned toward her, still laughing. "What are you going to do? Hit me?"

Hero was trembling. She clenched her fist, but Danny caught her arm. "She won't have to. Because I will. Cut it out."

He was still smiling, but his eyes had that hard look, the one that reminded Hero of his father. She jerked free and walked away from the corner, her cheeks burning. When she heard Danny behind her, she walked faster.

"Hero, wait up."

She wanted to keep going; she wanted to ignore him. But she realized with a start that he had called her Hero, not Netherfield. She glanced over her shoulder, quickening her pace.

"What?"

"Look, I . . ."

"What's wrong with you?" she hissed at him, lowering her voice. "Why are you acting so weird? We found the diamond! We have to tell Mrs. Roth."

He caught up to her. "The thing is . . ." His voice trailed off and he looked away again.

"What? What is it? We have to give it to her." Hero scanned his face, unable to read his expression.

"We can't," he said finally.

"Why?"

Hero stared at him. They were at Mrs. Roth's now, just at the gate. Hero couldn't stand the pleading look in his eyes. She felt a surge of panic.

"You didn't—you didn't tell your dad about it, did you?"

"No . . ."

"Then what? What's the matter? Where's the diamond?"

"I . . ."

Hero stiffened, then shivered a little. Suddenly she knew. Without his saying anything. He didn't have it. She felt a wide pit open in her stomach, and all her nervous happiness vanished inside.

"Danny, just tell me. Whatever it is," Hero said slowly.

He was still watching her with that terrible hopeful look in his eyes. "I don't have it. I . . ." He swallowed.

"I took it to the post office this morning. I sent the diamond to my mom."

This was so unexpected that Hero could only stare at him. "What?"

"I sent it to my mom."

"But . . . why?"

Just then the door swung open, and Mrs. Roth stepped onto the porch. She held out her arms to them. "Oh, finally, you're here! Come in, come in. I could barely sleep last night. What happened? Did you find it? Is the Murphy diamond found at last?"

CHAPTER 27

Hero looked from Danny to Mrs. Roth and back again. She couldn't think what to do, what to say. She longed to hurtle back to last night, to that one bright moment on the porch with Danny, when the diamond had tumbled into her palm. Except this time, she wanted Mrs. Roth to be there, too.

Danny's cheeks were flushed, and he shifted from one foot to the other. He shot a brief, miserable glance at Hero, then stared at the ground. Hero took a deep breath. Squaring her shoulders, she walked to the porch.

"Well, my heavens, what is it?" Mrs. Roth asked. "What's happened?"

Hero reached out and touched Mrs. Roth's arm, fingering the thin silk of her sleeve.

"We found it," she said softly.

Mrs. Roth's whole face changed. So many feelings chased across it that Hero drew back, a little afraid. Mrs. Roth pressed one hand to her cheek and sat down with a shudder on the top step.

"Oh, my dears," she whispered. "Hero. Daniel. I can't believe it. The Murphy diamond."

Danny crossed the path to the porch in a few swift steps. He stood in front of Mrs. Roth, his jaw tight. Hero saw that his sweatshirt was torn at the bottom, and he gripped it with both hands, twisting the hem.

"Miriam, listen. We don't have it," he said quietly. "I . . ."

When he didn't continue, Hero said it for him: "Danny sent it to his mother."

Mrs. Roth looked up, confused. "What? What do you mean? What has Daniel's mother got to do with this?"

"Nothing," Danny said. "Nothing. I just . . ." He crouched on the steps below her. "Listen. If we had the diamond, what could we do with it? You said yourself, Miriam, it doesn't belong to us. I mean, I know that from my dad. Ever since Mr. Murphy collected the insurance money, the diamond belongs to them, the insurance company. We'd—well, we'd have to turn it in."

Mrs. Roth continued to gaze at him. "But I don't understand. You gave it to your mother? I thought your mother was in California somewhere."

Hero couldn't bear the strange, intense look on Danny's face. It made her want to cry. She turned away, her eyes settling on the fading colors of the garden. She thought of how this place had seemed to her—lush and overflowing—when she met Mrs. Roth for the first time. Then she heard her own voice and it surprised her, how calm she sounded.

"Danny's mother's an actress in L.A. At least she's trying to be one. She doesn't have much money."

"She doesn't have any money," Danny corrected. "You need money to make it out there. You need classes, you need the right clothes, you need . . . money. I just thought, you know, we can't do anything with the diamond here. We'd have to give it to the police, to the insurance company. You don't even have the necklace, so—"

"The necklace," Mrs. Roth said softly.

Hero sat beside her and took her hand. "I know."

Danny looked at them in confusion. "What?"

Mrs. Roth looked at Hero. "I suppose he might as well know." She rose a little unsteadily and went into the house. She returned with the cardboard box and emptied its contents into Hero's outstretched palm.

"It's Mrs. Murphy's necklace," Hero explained, as she lifted it, sparkling in the sunlight. "The one that had the diamond in it. It's almost five hundred years old. Can you believe that?" She didn't want to make him feel worse, but she had to tell him. "We found out it belonged to Anne Boleyn—the wife of Henry VIII—and to Queen Elizabeth, and we even think . . ." Hero hesitated. How to explain the rest?

Mrs. Roth finished for her. "We think it proves the true identity of William Shakespeare. Imagine that, Daniel! William Shakespeare. We think Eleanor Murphy's ancestor, Edward de Vere, was the illegitimate son of Queen Elizabeth and the real William Shakespeare."

"What?" Danny said. "What are you talking about?" He looked at both of them in bewilderment. "You never told me you had the necklace, Miriam. Hero, you never told me any of this," he said accusingly.

"Daniel," Mrs. Roth said gently.

"But if I'd known . . ." Danny said. "I didn't know you had the necklace." He stared at the ground.

Mrs. Roth sighed and took both of his hands in hers, stilling their frantic twisting. The wrinkled hem of his sweatshirt flopped against his jeans. "Oh, Daniel."

Danny looked at the necklace in Hero's hand. "It's so small," he said. He turned apologetically to Hero.

"I should have asked you first. I should have talked to you about it. I thought you'd say no."

"Well, duh." Hero smiled a little. She thought of the diamond and closed her fist around the empty pendant. Gently she settled the necklace in the nest of tissue paper inside the box. "So what did you do with it, anyway? You just mailed it to her? How do you know it'll even get there?"

"Hey, Federal Express." Danny smiled, looking more like his old self. "I wrapped it in a sock."

Mrs. Roth stood slowly, resting her hand on the porch rail. She looked at the Netherfields' house for a minute, not saying anything. Danny watched her anxiously.

"Sorry, Miriam," he said quietly.

She closed her eyes and took a deep breath. When she opened them, she was smiling faintly. "Well." She turned to Hero and Danny. "Nothing quite turns out the way we expect, does it? But Daniel is right. The diamond didn't belong to us. I only wish . . ." She crossed the porch and stopped at the door. "I wish I could have seen it returned to the necklace."

"I know," Hero said.

Mrs. Roth looked at Danny, and her eyes were kind. "But you two found the Murphy diamond! You had it for a few hours at least. I'm sure there's much to tell, and I want to hear all of it. Come inside. It's chilly this morning."

◇ ◇ ◇

Hero and Danny followed her into the dark house. Mrs. Roth gestured to the worn furniture in the living room. "Sit down. I'll bring us some tea."

Hero moved a newspaper and a book from the sofa, settling into the cushions. She saw that the newspaper was folded open to the crossword puzzle and idly started working it in her head. *Put together,* she read; seven letters, starting with *C*. Combine? No, connect.

Danny remained standing, looking around the room with interest. "Hey, I've never been in here before," he said. "Cool map."

"Yes, Australia," Mrs. Roth called from the kitchen. "Now tell me about the diamond! Where did you find it?"

"It was in one of the lights, just like we thought," Danny said. They could hear the piercing whine of the teakettle.

"The porch light," Hero added. "The one we don't have a switch for. That's why no one ever found it before us."

"Really? That was clever of Arthur. An excellent

finding place." Mrs. Roth came into the room, carrying a tray of mugs and a plate of muffins.

"Cranberry," she said. "They're a little tart. So what made you look there?" She nudged the books and papers aside and set the tray on the coffee table.

Hero bit into a muffin and puckered her lips at the tang of the cranberries. "We looked pretty much everywhere else first," she said. With a twinge, she remembered the bedroom light crashing to the floor.

Danny walked behind the sofa, squinting at the array of photographs covering the wall. "We were about to give up," he said.

Mrs. Roth sipped her tea. "But you didn't. You kept looking, as I knew you would. Neither of you is easily deterred. Tell me about finding it."

"Well," Hero began. "Danny was about to leave because it was so late, and my parents were coming back soon, and we—"

"We sort of thought of it at the same time. It was right above us—the light—and we looked up and figured the diamond might be there. Then Hero said it didn't have a switch—"

"And then we just knew it had to be there. So Danny helped me stand on the rail, and we got the light down—"

"And there it was. Inside the glass," Danny finished.

Mrs. Roth shook her head in amazement. "And it's been there all along! Right under our noses. Or over them, I suppose. What did you think of it? Oh, Hero, was it beautiful?"

"Yes," Hero said reverently. She thought of the diamond, reflecting tiny splinters of light in her hand. "It was sort of dirty, but even in the dark, it still sparkled."

"Hey," said Danny. They both turned to him. He was leaning close to one of the pictures, rubbing the dust off the glass with his sleeve. "Hey, this looks like my mom."

Mrs. Roth smiled. "Does it? Is she blond, like you? That's Anna's school picture from her junior year. The last one I have of her."

"No," Danny said, still staring at the photo. "What I mean is . . . this *is* my mom."

CHAPTER 28

Hero scrambled onto her knees and leaned over the back of the couch. For a minute, she couldn't understand what Danny was saying. But then she saw the photograph. She gasped. The girl in the picture had Danny's blond hair and, more strikingly, his eyes, though it was hard to read their expression because they glanced away from the camera. Her mouth was drawn and pinched, not Danny's wide grin. But there was no doubt. She looked so much like Danny she had to be his mother.

Mrs. Roth walked over to Danny. "You must be mistaken," she said gently.

Danny's face was flushed. His eyes were riveted to the picture. He couldn't seem to see anything else. "No, listen. I know it doesn't make sense. But it's my mom. This is my mom."

Mrs. Roth stared at him. "That isn't possible."

The silence in the room filled Hero's ears. Suddenly she understood. She felt a shiver run through her whole body. Anna was Danny's mother. Of course it was true. All at once she saw that it did make sense. It made more sense than anything else.

"Mrs. Roth," Hero whispered. "The finding place! You and Danny both called it that, but I thought it was just a coincidence."

Mrs. Roth turned to the photo. Her voice sounded small and far away. "But how can that be?"

"And the postcard Anna sent you," Hero continued urgently, "saying she'd had a baby. The baby was Danny!"

Mrs. Roth reached out to touch the glass, running her fingers lightly across the girl's face. Hero could tell it was something she'd done many times.

"Oh, Mrs. Roth," she breathed. "Your Anna is Danny's mother. He's your grandson." Her words echoed through the still room.

The color drained from Mrs. Roth's face and she reached for the back of the sofa. Hero thought for a minute she might faint. But she kept staring at the photo, at the girl whose eyes always darted away.

Hero shook her head, still puzzled. But was that

possible? Mrs. Roth and Danny's mother had lived in the same small town and never met? She turned to Danny. "But, Danny, you all lived here together, in the same town. How did you . . . why didn't you ever find one another?"

Danny dragged his gaze away from the photo and turned to Hero. "No," he said slowly. "We used to live in D.C., right in the city. We moved out here when my mom left. The funny thing is, my dad said she picked it. The town, I mean. They'd been talking about moving out of the city, and she wanted a small town. She said it would be a good place for me to grow up. And then, after she left for California, my dad moved us here anyway."

Hero touched Mrs. Roth's arm. She wanted somehow to connect, to make it all fit together. "Do you think she knew? Mrs. Roth, do you think Anna knew you were here?"

Mrs. Roth kept stroking the glass of the picture, her eyes shining with tears. She seemed not to hear them. "Oh, Anna," she whispered. "You were so close. You were so close all the time. How can it be I never found you?"

Hero saw that Danny was looking at Mrs. Roth strangely. "You found me," he said quietly.

Mrs. Roth finally turned to them, her face pale and wet. She stared at Danny, hearing him for the first time. Her whole body shook. She pulled him tightly to her, and Danny's hands rose slowly to touch her shoulders.

CHAPTER 29

The rest of the afternoon had the strange feel of a dream, with people doing unexpected things that somehow seemed perfectly natural. Mrs. Roth looked happier than Hero had ever seen her, her eyes bright with pleasure, her hands reaching eagerly to pat Danny's face or squeeze Hero's arm. Danny appeared to be in shock, but Hero noticed that he put up with it all, never pulling back from her touch. Even though Hero herself was talking and eating muffins and drinking cup after cup of tea, she felt like she was watching it all from a great distance, the final scene in a play.

They sat in the darkening living room until almost suppertime, talking about what had happened. Mostly they talked about Anna. Mrs. Roth told them every small thing she could remember. She brought out two faded albums of photographs, and together they leaned over them, peering through the yellowing cellophane at Anna eating birthday cake, Anna learning to ride a bike, Anna holding a neighbor's kitten. They watched her hair grow long and short again, watched her gap-toothed smile change, filled with teeth too big for her face. They saw dance recitals and family outings and softball games. It was strange to see Mrs. Roth embedded in this family, Hero thought. Mrs. Roth always seemed so distinctly alone.

"There aren't many of Arthur. He took all the pictures," Mrs. Roth said. "But, look, here he is." She pointed to a middle-aged man with curly brown hair and glasses.

Hero looked at him with interest. He was nothing like the Mr. Murphy of her imagination, the one she had pictured over and over hiding the diamond. He looked ordinary, like one of the neighbors. She realized that all of it looked ordinary, just the ordinary things families did, exactly like the photos in her parents' albums at home.

"So what happened?" she asked. "What made Anna leave?"

Mrs. Roth sat back, sliding the album deeper into her lap. She didn't say anything.

Danny frowned at Hero. "Nothing made her leave. She just left, right?"

Mrs. Roth flipped the pages back to the beginning of the album, to the little girl with white-blond hair and Danny's eyes.

"I'm not sure even Anna would know the answer to that," she said. "I blamed myself for a while. As hard as that was, somehow it was easier than not having any reason at all."

Danny looked at her, not saying anything.

At that moment the phone rang. Mrs. Roth handed the album to Danny and hurried into the kitchen to answer it. Hero could hear her apologizing.

"Oh, of course, I'm sorry. She's been here all day. We completely lost track of the time. She'll come right now."

Hero stood up. "I guess I have to go." Danny nodded, barely paying attention. He was still looking through the pictures.

Mrs. Roth walked over to a lamp and switched it on, bathing them in light. "Hero, that was your mother. Dinner is on the table." She rested her hand on Danny's shoulder. "I suppose you should go too, Daniel, before your father starts to worry."

"I can stay awhile longer," Danny said quickly. "He's at the station till eight tonight."

"Really? We can have dinner together then. That would be lovely. Let me see what I have for us."

As Mrs. Roth returned to the kitchen, Hero picked up her sweater and tugged open the front door. "See you later, Danny."

"See you, Hero." He didn't look up, his eyes gliding steadily over the pages of the album. Hero smiled to herself, stepping into the cool evening air.

⟡ ⟡ ⟡

At the Netherfield house, Hero's mother was serving plates at the stove while Beatrice clunked batches of silverware on the table.

"Hey!" she said when Hero walked in. "What were you doing in my room?"

Hero remembered the broken light and shook her head quickly at her sister.

Their mother looked at them questioningly. Beatrice frowned at Hero and said reluctantly, "Hero's been going through my clothes."

"Well, you do that often enough to her."

After dinner, Hero did the dishes while Beatrice sat on the counter watching her. As soon as their parents left the kitchen, Beatrice demanded, "So what were you doing up there? You broke my light into a jillion pieces."

Hero hesitated, scraping potatoes into the sink.

"Come on, Hero. Just tell me. What's the big

secret? You think I don't know something's going on? All the time you're spending over at Mrs. Roth's? And Danny? Something's going on with Danny."

"Not what you think," Hero said. "It's not what anyone thinks."

"Then tell me."

Hero sighed. It was over now, anyway. There was no secret to keep anymore. She stuffed a fistful of forks into the dishwasher rack and turned to Beatrice. "You can't tell."

"I won't."

"You can't tell anyone, not Kelly, not anyone."

"I won't, okay? I promise."

"It's the diamond. Danny and I . . ." Hero took a deep breath. "We found the Murphy diamond."

Beatrice looked at her blankly. "What diamond?"

Hero laughed suddenly, thinking how strange it was that the diamond had dominated her life for weeks—the only thing she could think about—and Triss didn't even know what it was. She slammed the dishwasher door, flipped the lock, and wiped her hands on her jeans.

"Okay," she said. "I'll start at the beginning. Remember the day before school started, when Mom asked me to take back those clippers she borrowed from Mrs. Roth?"

And then she proceeded to tell the story, about the Murphys and the necklace, about Anne Boleyn and Queen Elizabeth, about Edward de Vere and Shakespeare, about the diamond and the finding place. Beatrice listened, at first only curious, then surprised, then amazed. But Hero stopped short when she came to the part about Anna being Mrs. Roth's daughter. It didn't seem like that was hers to tell.

"So it's gone now? Danny's mother has it?" Beatrice asked in disbelief.

Hero nodded.

"Wow. You must be pretty mad at him."

Hero shook her head. "Not really. I don't know. Nothing ever turns out the way you expect."

Their father suddenly appeared in the kitchen doorway, looking annoyed. "Anything you girls want to tell me about the light in Beatrice's room?"

Hero and Beatrice exchanged glances. "No," they answered simultaneously.

He frowned. "These are the original fixtures, you know. Irreplaceable."

Beatrice took a breath. "The bulb went out, and we were trying to change it," she offered hopefully.

"Beatrice, you've never changed a lightbulb in your life. If you're going to lie to me, at least put some effort into making it more believable."

Hero swallowed. "It was my fault," she said. "I was jumping on the bed. Sorry, Dad."

Her father rolled his eyes in disgust. "Now that I believe. For pity's sake, Hero. You're twelve years old." He disappeared down the hallway, grumbling.

Beatrice waited till he was out of earshot, then hopped down from the counter. "But the diamond," she said. "What's Danny's mom going to do with it?"

"I don't know." Hero paused. "I don't know anything about her."

She walked to the window and looked at Mrs. Roth's house. She could see a tiny square of light over the top of the fence. It must be the light from the kitchen window, she decided. She pictured Mrs. Roth and Danny together at the table, eating and talking. They would have so much to tell each other. Hero suddenly felt a warm swell of happiness that had nothing to do with herself.

CHAPTER 30

The next week passed quickly. Hero floated through the days at school, oblivious to everything but an overwhelming urge to be back at Mrs. Roth's with Danny. They met there every day after school. Sometimes, if Danny was late, she and Mrs. Roth worked the crossword puzzle. But mostly it was the three of them, sitting on the porch if it was warm enough or in the dark, cluttered living room, talking about the strange series of events that had brought them all together.

"That first day," Hero said to Mrs. Roth, "if you hadn't told me about the diamond, I never would have come back here. I mean, unless my mom made me."

"And if you hadn't started coming here, I probably wouldn't have either," Danny added.

Hero smiled shyly. "And then we never would have found out about the necklace or Anne Boleyn or Queen Elizabeth or Shakespeare . . . or Anna." She turned to Danny. "Has she called you yet?" They had been waiting all week for some word, some acknowledgment. But there'd been none.

Danny shook his head. "But she doesn't call much. I could try and call her." He hesitated. "My dad doesn't really like me to."

"You'll hear from her," Mrs. Roth said confidently. They both turned to her. "I feel sure of it. I wrote to her, you know."

"You did?" Hero looked at her in astonishment.

"Oh, yes, of course, right away. Daniel gave me her address."

"Did you tell her about the diamond?"

Mrs. Roth frowned. "That wasn't why I wrote. There was so much else to say."

Danny sighed. "I don't know, Miriam. I wouldn't get your hopes up. She's not much for writing letters either."

"We'll hear from her," Mrs. Roth said again decisively. She brushed her hands together. "And now we have something more pressing to discuss. I want to have a little get-together on Friday. Your family, Hero, and your father, Danny. After all, he is my son-in-law.

I'll call and invite them this afternoon. Would you two come over after school to help me get everything ready?"

The question made Hero smile, since they came every day anyway. "Sure," she said. "But what's the party for?"

Mrs. Roth looked at her in surprise. "I want to celebrate," she said. "I want to celebrate our finding one another."

✧ ✧ ✧

And so, on Friday, when the dismissal bell rang at school, Hero quickly packed her things and headed for the bus. She was a little nervous about seeing Danny's father again. And she felt strange, somehow, at the thought of her parents and Beatrice at Mrs. Roth's. It was a place she wasn't used to sharing.

As she was waiting in line for the bus, she heard a voice behind her.

"You forgot your book." It was the red-haired girl, Tory, the one with the dog named Hero. She was holding the battered green book of Shakespeare from Mrs. Roth. Hero looked at it in surprise.

"Oh, thanks," she said, puzzled. "I didn't know I brought that to school." It must have been with her Language Arts book on her nightstand and she'd accidentally slipped it into her backpack. She took it carefully, unzipping the top of her pack.

"What is it anyway?" Tory asked. "It looks really old."

Hero felt herself blushing. She would seem even more of a freak if the other kids found out she read Shakespeare. But then she thought about what Beatrice had said, about not raising her hand in class even though she recognized the quote. Hero shrugged.

"It's a Shakespeare book a friend gave me," she said. "Because one of the plays has a girl named Hero in it, and that's who I'm named for."

"Oh," said Tory.

Hero turned back to the line, impatient for the bus to arrive. But she realized Tory was still standing there, looking at her expectantly.

"Uh, thanks for finding it," Hero said.

"No problem." Tory twisted a strand of hair. "If you want, you could come over today. My mom's picking me up, so she can give us a ride."

Hero looked at her in surprise. She hesitated. "I can't. I have plans. Sorry."

"Oh, okay," Tory glanced away. "Never mind. I'd better go to pickup."

Hero took a breath. "I could come over some other time," she said. "Maybe next week?"

Tory smiled at her. "I have to ask my mom. I'll let you know."

"Okay." Hero watched her hurry down the hall, feeling a mixture of curiosity and amazement. She wasn't sure which surprised her more: that Tory had asked her over or that she'd been willing to go. Then the bus line started moving toward the doors, and she swung her backpack over her shoulder, running to catch up.

CHAPTER 31

When the bus stopped, Hero followed Aaron down the steps. Ben was standing at the corner. He glanced at Hero appraisingly, then said to Aaron, "Come on. Mom's waiting for you. You're going to the doctor for your checkup."

Aaron's face crumpled. "Will I get a shot? Last time I got a shot. Will they give me a shot this time?"

"Yep," said Ben. "With one of those great big needles like they use on horses."

Aaron's breath turned ragged, and he grabbed Hero's hand. "Is he right? Are they going to give me a shot?"

Hero glared at Ben in disgust. She crouched down next to Aaron. "How old are you?"

"Six," he whimpered.

"I don't think you'll get a shot. You get a lot of shots before you start school, but after that they just check your height and that kind of thing."

"Really?" He turned back to Ben. "Is she right?"

Ben looked at Hero, then grinned suddenly. "Yeah. I'm not messing with her. Come on, you can ride on my back." He grabbed Aaron's backpack. "Boost him up," he told Hero.

Hero lifted Aaron high enough to wrap his arms around his brother's neck, and watched Ben jog toward their driveway with Aaron's skinny legs flapping around Ben's waist. She heard Ben say, "But you know, if you don't get a shot, you don't get a lollipop either." She smiled as Aaron began to whine in protest.

⋄ ⋄ ⋄

When she reached Mrs. Roth's, she saw Danny in the garden. He was using the clippers to shear a thicket of dead brown stalks in the flower bed next to the fence.

He looked up eagerly when Hero came through the gate. "Okay, Miriam, she's here. Now show us!"

"What?" Hero asked.

"Something came in the mail, but Miriam made me wait till you got here to see it."

Mrs. Roth rose, flushed and smiling, from the steps. "All right, I'll get it." As she left the porch, Hero looked at Danny.

"From your mom? Did your mom finally write back?"

"I don't know. But it must be about the diamond." He tossed down the clippers and bounded up the steps with Hero.

Mrs. Roth returned to the porch, carrying a bulky white cardboard envelope. "Hey," said Danny. "That looks familiar."

Smiling at him, she slid her hand in one end and they heard rustling. She slowly drew it out, opening her fingers to reveal the Murphy diamond.

Hero caught her breath. It rested in the center of Mrs. Roth's hand, all light and angles, glowing in the afternoon sun. Danny looked crestfallen. "She sent it back," he said quietly. "I can't believe she sent it back."

"It wasn't hers to keep," Mrs. Roth said gently.

Hero reached out to touch it, skating her finger over the glassy surface.

"But it's not ours either. What do we do now?"

Mrs. Roth handed the diamond to Hero, who promptly curled her fingers around it. "Anna sent a letter. I want to read it to you." She reached back into the envelope and pulled out a folded piece of notebook paper. Hero could see small, jagged script crowding the page. Mrs. Roth smoothed it over her lap and began reading.

"Dear Mia—"

"Mia?" Hero asked.

"What she always called me," Mrs. Roth explained. "Now listen.

"Dear Mia,

I can't keep this. Please put it back where it belongs. I don't know how Danny got it, but I don't want him to get in trouble.

Take care of him for me. I wish I could be with him, but I can't. He's a good kid. Thanks for your letter, maybe I'll write more when I have time.

I think about you a lot, about all that's happened, but it's like they say, you can't change the past."

Mrs. Roth flattened the letter on her lap. "There's one more thing," she said quietly. Clearing her throat, she read:

"And give Danny this picture for me."

She paused and looked at Danny, who was staring at the porch, tugging the bottom of his shirt. She shook the envelope, and a creased photograph fell into her lap. She gave it to Danny. Hero could see that it was a picture of a woman and a little boy. The woman was blond and pretty. Her head was turned, laughing at the boy, whose hands she held stretched out as far as they would go. The boy was smiling at the camera, a wide easy grin that even now was completely Danny's own.

"Read the back," Mrs. Roth said quietly. Danny shook his head, sucking in his breath. He handed the picture to Hero.

She looked at him questioningly, but when he nodded, she turned it over and read aloud the words printed carefully across the back:

"My heart, my hope
My soul, my smile

My held and whole
Beloved child."

Hero looked at Mrs. Roth. "Is that a quote from something?"

Mrs. Roth sighed, smiling a little. "It's from a song I used to sing to Anna before she went to sleep. I can't believe she remembered it."

Danny took the photo. They sat in silence, staring at it, the words of the letter echoing in the air between them. Hero loosened her fingers to look at the diamond.

"So what do we do now?" Danny asked finally.

"We'll have to call the police eventually," said Mrs. Roth. "But I don't think we have to do that right away. Let's put it back first, shall we?"

Mrs. Roth went into the house. When she returned, she had the necklace draped across her palm. She took the diamond from Hero and gently pressed it into the pendant. "It will need to be reset properly," she said. "But, here. Look." The pearls and rubies marched unstoppably toward the pendant, which hung at the bottom, now beautifully complete.

"Wow," Danny said.

Hero could only stare at it. She thought of the

necklace's long journey, from brave, persecuted Anne Boleyn to her daughter, Elizabeth, trapped in her prison room, too scared to wear her mother's pendant but clever enough to use its diamond to scratch a poem on the window glass. Then to Edward de Vere, maybe Elizabeth's son and the secret Shakespeare. And then through the Vere family to Eleanor Murphy, who died not knowing the necklace's history and secrets.

And now, finally, to the three of them, who knew its secrets but would have no choice but to give it up.

Mrs. Roth handed the necklace to Hero. "Put it on, my dear," she said softly.

Hero hesitated, then took it gingerly and unclasped it, fitting it around her throat. She felt the pendant plunk against her chest as she ran her fingers over the jeweled chain.

"Isn't it lovely?" Mrs. Roth smiled with satisfaction.

They sat in silence, staring at the diamond. Hero felt transformed by it.

Danny sighed. "Do we have to give it to the police? What a waste."

"Hey," Hero said suddenly. "I know what we can do! We'll tell my dad. We'll tell him the whole story. He'll be so excited. I mean, to see the necklace that proves who Shakespeare really was. And the other night, he said that the Maxwell buys lots of things besides manuscripts and old books. Don't you think they'd want something like this?" She touched the diamond. "They can pay the insurance company for the diamond, and then the diamond and the necklace can stay together, at the Maxwell."

Mrs. Roth clapped her hands together. "What an excellent idea! Perhaps everything will work out after all. If the necklace ends up at the Maxwell, we can always go there to look at it." She smiled with satisfaction. "'Our remedies oft in ourselves do lie.'"

Hero smiled back at her. "Shakespeare?"

"Of course."

Danny shook his head. "Now here's what I don't get: How could somebody write something five hundred years ago and it still makes sense today?"

Mrs. Roth rose slowly from the steps, her eyes lingering on the necklace. "That's the real mystery, isn't it? Not whether he was a common merchant or the queen's son, but how he could understand so much about human nature. And write about it in a way that still rings true, all these years later." She smiled at them. "That's Shakespeare's secret. And I suppose we'll never figure it out."

She opened the door. "Now, my friends, we need to start getting ready for our guests. Danny, pick up those clippers and put them by the side of the house, will you?"

Mrs. Roth disappeared inside. Hero stayed on the steps, watching Danny in the garden. Past the fence, in her own driveway, she saw Beatrice's friend Kelly walking toward the house. Kelly looked over at them and came to the fence. "Danny?" she called.

Danny glanced up, wiping his hands on his jeans. "Hey," he said.

Kelly smiled at him, tossing her hair. "What are you doing?"

"Hanging out," Danny said.

Kelly shot a quick glance at Hero. "Who with?"

Danny sat back on his heels and looked from Kelly to Hero, as if he didn't understand what was going on but still found it funny. "Hero," he said. "I'm hanging out with Hero."

Hero felt a warm tingling spread through her.

Kelly snorted and started to say something, then stopped. "Well, why don't you come over later?"

"I can't," Danny said. "I'm going to be here for a while."

Kelly pursed her lips. "See you at school," she said finally, and turned back toward the Netherfields' house.

Danny stood up, slapping the dirt off his jeans. He

climbed the steps of the porch. The afternoon sun slanted over him, and Hero had to shield her eyes with her hand to see his face. "Is it weird for you?" she asked. "All the stuff with your mom?"

He looked down at her, smiling his easy smile. "The stuff with my mom has always been weird. You won't believe this, but the letter, and the picture she sent . . . that kind of makes it less weird."

Hero nodded. "I believe it."

She unzipped her backpack and pulled out the green book.

"What's that?" Danny asked.

"A book of Shakespeare's plays," Hero said, scanning the table of contents. "Mrs. Roth gave it to me. I'm going to read the one about the girl named Hero. *Much Ado About Nothing.*"

Danny laughed. "Well, yeah, that's the story of our lives." Hero liked the way he said "our." He pulled open the door. "You coming?"

"In a minute."

As the door banged shut, Hero leaned against the porch railing and opened the book across her lap. She smoothed the pages. With one hand she stroked the diamond, absently touching the chain.

Then she began to read.

AUTHOR'S NOTE

While the characters and plot of this book are entirely fictitious, all the historical figures and details are true, with the exception of the necklace. The necklace never existed, but I modeled it (and the diamond) on jewelry of the period.

There is no proof that Edward de Vere, the seventeenth Earl of Oxford, was the real author of Shakespeare's plays. But that theory has gained momentum recently—as Hero's father relates—with the discovery that Oxford's Bible contains marked passages corresponding with key verses in the plays.

For the most part, scholars still favor the man from Stratford as the true Shakespeare. However, both the Stratfordians and the Oxfordians (as the two camps are known) believe that a significant relationship between Elizabeth I and Edward de Vere would further the case for Oxford. Any conspiracy to conceal Shakespeare's true identity most likely depended on the blessing of the queen herself. While there is no proof that Edward de Vere was the son of Elizabeth I, there is clear evidence of a connection between them, and the notion that he might have been either her lover or her son continues to be discussed.

The case for Edward de Vere as Shakespeare is compelling. Edward de Vere's purported nickname at court was "Spear-shaker," perhaps stemming from his skill in tournaments or from his coat of arms, which depicted a lion brandishing a spear. While his published poetry is considered inferior to Shakespeare's, scholars note that certain unusual poetic forms occur in both Oxford's work and Shakespeare's, but not in the poetry of their contemporaries.

Moreover, many details of Edward de Vere's life coincide intriguingly with aspects of Shakespeare's plays. His travels to Italy might have influenced the settings of *The Merchant of Venice* and *Othello*. His notorious tennis feud with another young courtier appears to be referenced in *Hamlet*. And in the same play, the character Polonius is considered a parody of Oxford's father-in-law, William Cecil, Lord Burghley.

The biggest argument against Edward de Vere as the true Shakespeare is the fact that several of Shakespeare's plays are believed to have been written after Oxford's death in 1604. However, even the most ardent Stratfordians admit that the dating of the plays is uncertain.

What do I think? As a historian, I don't find the evidence to be complete enough—yet—to topple the man from Stratford from his literary pedestal. But as a novelist, I am more convinced. Writing this book reminded me of what I love so much about history. The past offers up its gifts: Anne Boleyn's speech on Tower Green, the scandal that sent Elizabeth in a cloud of shame from her stepmother's house, the poem she wrote with a diamond on her prison window, and the vague circumstances of Edward de Vere's birth and close relationship to the queen. But it is left to us—as readers, explorers, detectives, and storytellers—to see the patterns, to make the connections. Perhaps the answer to the mystery of Shakespeare's true identity is best found in the words of the Bard himself:

> *All the world's a stage,*
> *And all the men and women merely players.*
> *They have their exits and their entrances;*
> *And one man in his time plays many parts.*

William Shakespeare *Anne Boleyn*

Queen Elizabeth I *Edward de Vere*

HISTORICAL TIMELINE

1532 Henry VIII grants his mistress, Anne Boleyn, the title of Marquess of Pembroke and its falcon crest.

1533 Anne Boleyn weds Henry VIII; Elizabeth I is born.

1536 Anne Boleyn is executed for treason on Tower Green.

1547 Henry VIII dies.

1548 Elizabeth is evicted from the house of her stepmother Catherine Parr amidst rumors of sexual impropriety involving Catherine Parr's second husband, Lord Admiral Thomas Seymour.

1550 Edward de Vere is born.

1554 Elizabeth is accused of treason by Queen Mary I and arrested and imprisoned at Woodstock; she uses a diamond to write poetry on her prison window.

1558 Elizabeth becomes Queen of England; Edward de Vere becomes a ward of the court and a great favorite of the queen a few years later.

1564 William Shakespeare of Stratford is born.

1576 Edward de Vere's poetry is published; he is ranked first among Elizabeth I's courtier poets by contemporary critics.

1586 Elizabeth I begins paying Edward de Vere an annual pension of 1,000 pounds.

1589–1613 Shakespeare's plays are written and performed; most are not published until twenty years later.

1603 Elizabeth I dies.

1604 Edward de Vere dies.

1616 William Shakespeare dies.

ACKNOWLEDGMENTS

Writing may seem a solitary act, but in reality it depends on the goodwill and generosity, patience and support of so many others. It is a privilege to thank the following people for their many contributions to this book:

- First, last, and always, my amazing family: my husband, Ward Wheeler, and my children, Zoe, Harry, and Grace. They put up with a lot in order for this book to be written, and incredibly, they seem to feel it was worth it.
- Christy Ottaviano, my gifted editor, who graced this project with a keen eye and a sure touch, asking all the right questions and wisely letting me find my own answers.
- My writing group—Claire Carlson, Anne Gaston, Laurie Krebs, Mary Reilly, and Peggy Thomas—who began this journey with me and were peerless traveling companions: exceptional readers, writers, and friends.
- Patricia Reilly Giff, whose generosity as a teacher and colleague is legendary in the field, and whose many insights guided me through a first draft of this novel in her class at the Dinosaur's Paw.
- Liza Pulitzer Voges, who believed in the story and found it the right home.
- Steven Malk, who offered thoughtful advice and encouragement as the book made its way into the world.
- And finally, my talented company of readers, fact-checkers, and friends who lent this manuscript their valuable

perspectives as historians, writers, mystery buffs, legal experts, artists, gardeners, jewelry appraisers, English teachers, middle-school parents, and above all, lovers of fiction: Pamela Benepe, Barbara Broach, Bill Broach, Mary Broach, Jane Burns, Laura Forte, the staff at Michael Goldstein Antique Diamonds, Jane Kamensky, Carolyn Meek, Carol Sheriff, and Susanne and David Smith. I am especially indebted to my middle-school readers: Sophie and Julia Broach, Alexis and Taylor Smith, Ellen and Jane Urheim, James Wayne, and Zoe Wheeler.